The Adventures of the San Francisco Listener Thieves

Boyd E. Smith

Copyright © 1998 Boyd E. Smith
All rights reserved.
ISBN-13: 978-0615525075 (NFS)
ISBN-10: 0615525075

THE ADVENTURES OF THE SAN FRANCISCO LISTENER THIEVES

Boyd E. Smith

Year 2000 San Francisco: Friday 8:00 AM, October twenty-fourth, one week before Halloween. Channel 6 morning news report in progress from a converted office building: "Enthusiastic volunteers at the Ross for Mayor headquarters are already busy preparing a last minute mailing blitz for the primary. Their skillfully engineered message assures the voters that this candidate will be honest and productive for the people of San Francisco, the two qualities their main opponent, incumbent candidate Larry Bennard, has been faulted for repeatedly by his critics. The high level of enthusiasm here today has only been enhanced by the Chronicle's poll last night showing Ross and Bennard, neck and neck among the voters. There remains a mere two percent difference between them with Frank Ross standing to gain the majority of the swing votes after the primary. Candidate Ross arrives early at his headquarters every morning and takes the time to individually thank his volunteers personally."

The camera shifted to the mayoral hopeful chatting with his supporters.

"Good morning, people," Frank smiled intensely, "I just want to thank you for your support once more. Without you, this campaign wouldn't stand a chance. Because of your continued vigilance, we're going to win this election." The supporters' enthusiastic applause followed his encouraging words.

Frank put his hand on the shoulder of a young African-American volunteer and reached out to shake the hand of a silver-haired lady as the camera panned the room filled with normal middle-class people. Several newspaper photographers took photos concluding the morning news conference. The political consultants thanked the news crews for their early morning arrival as they then bolted out the door to their next stories.

"Jimmy, come here," Frank motioned at the reporter, waving his hand as the light on top of the camera went out indicating they were off air. "Thanks again everyone," Frank Ross kissed the old lady on the forehead before turning his full attention to the media reporter. "Jimmy, your support won't go unnoticed. I can't thank you enough for getting behind us at this crucial time. I'll see you at the press conference this afternoon...or are you off tonight?"

"No, it'll be me," he said, folding up his notepad and sticking it in his already stuffed bag. Frank Ross's political consultant Jack Swanson, who was waiting in the wings behind the camera, stepped forward. "Hey, Jimmy," he said, concerned, "We've already been talking to your producer most the morning on the phone. We need to buy air time for tomorrow, a few hours before the primary."

"Yes, they were expecting that. We can only hold the time slot 'til tonight though. Then we have to book it with another advertiser."

"Don't do that!" Jack said forcefully in reply, "We'll have the money to you by ten tonight. I give you my word."

"We'll hold it not one minute longer than ten. Please understand Jack, you have to come through by then. You know we're really going out on a limb for you guys to win this election. If you lose, it's going to be difficult for us to get any coverage of the administration at all. On top of that, we know Mayor Bennard will leverage his little bullshit threats against our advertisers, to pour salt on our wounds. He's done it already. That's one of the reasons we're so antagonistic to him."

"Fuck Bennard," Jack said loudly, then quickly dropped his tone not wishing to upset any of his volunteer staff. "We're going to stomp them into the ground," he whispered to Jimmy cupping his hand around his mouth. Grabbing Jimmy by the arm and walking him out of the crowd he continued to talk, "We're going to run them out of this city—Is that clear enough?—and your channel will get all the breaking news, total access, whatever you need just like channel three does now. Just stick with us Jimmy!" Jack looked straight into his eyes for assurance.

"Yeah..., OK," Jimmy replied as he grabbed his folder off the desk and darted out the door, his camera man following right behind him.

Frank, surrounded by his supporters, talked to them in his autopilot response mode, nodding his head and saying "yes," or responding with general comments. "We'll see what we can do." "Let's get into office first, and we'll take care of all these problems." "Yes, that's a concern of mine also, and something will be done."

Jack Swanson grabbed him by the back of his coat arm and pulled him away. "Sorry folks, we've got an election we've got to win. Lots of commitments to make. Please talk to Diane about everybody getting rides down to the press conference this afternoon. We need a big crowd of screaming supporters to rock the Union Hall." Before anybody could respond, Jack pushed his candidate up the stairs to the campaign staff area located on the second floor of the complex. The two walked briskly to the mayoral candidate's office, navigating the maze of desks thrown together on short notice, crammed with staff all working feverishly. The second floor was exclusively for the paid campaign workers, no time was wasted being polite or cheery with them.

Frank unlocked the door and went into his office, one of the only three walled off spaces upstairs. The other two areas were Jack Swanson's office and the restroom.

"We need money," Jack said, dispensing with any formality while pulling the door to Frank's office shut.

Downstairs, Diane, a neatly dressed

heavy-set lady, was in charge of the volunteers. The sleeves on her denim shirt were rolled up as if to show she was working hard. She gave orders to the volunteers in a childish tone like one would talk to grade-schoolers, "Now, everyone, we need these five hundred envelopes addressed, so we can mail them tonight. And then... we need all of you," Diane's voice raised slightly, "to meet at the rally, that's three thirty, in the Union Hall, and make as much noise as you possibly can."

Some of the volunteers glanced at each other with annoyed looks, but put up with the coddling. It was better than being talked down to like the paid workers endured upstairs.

In the main office behind closed doors, Frank Ross relaxed in his large leather reclining chair after removing his coat and loosening his tie. Jack Swanson didn't bother to sit down, but paced around the front half of the office. His reputation as a pit-bull of a political consultant was well deserved. The two stared at each other briefly, but Jack said nothing.

"Just call Bill, damn it!" Frank shouted pointedly at Jack. "He'll give you cash, and it will be here in less than an hour."

"I don't want to be involved with him!" Jack rubbed his forehead as he paced, gesturing agitatedly with his other hand, "One of his stupid puppets."

"You'll do what I say, got it? Without Bill Shoeghit this campaign wouldn't even be here."

"We're already into him for over five-hundred thousand dollars..."

"Then what's another hundred? In fact, what's another two-hundred thousand? We can't do anything if we're not elected, so you might as well play with all the parties."

"You already accepted too much from him. He'll run you and me around 'til we can't stand it anymore."

"I'll handle him... Now *do* it!... Leave me alone."

Jack said nothing, turned and walked out of the office pulling the door firmly shut. His dislike for Bill Shoeghit was expansive, but his paycheck was expansive too. Expansive enough to ignore vendettas. At least at the moment. The spoils of war only go to the victor and about a million in bonuses were his to be had if he could get Frank Ross elected. If he lost the election, Jack just spent nine months in vain. Even worse, he would accumulate a chink in his perfect, unsullied record of victories. Another big win, and his price for consulting would go astronomically high in the paid political consultant arena.

Downstairs Diana encouraged her volunteers to keep busy with their menial tasks. Each one went about work a little differently than the next. Some listened to headphones. Some chatted in small groups. Some just drifted into their own little world as they did the mindless addressing and stamping of the envelopes. At the end of one of the long fold-out tables, not in any of the cliques, working alone with his headphones on, sat a bearded gentleman with long brown hair and crystal blue eyes. The seemingly content volunteer was Steve Armstrong. Master Thief. Chief perpetrator of his self-invented San Francisco Listener Thieves' Guild. The most cunning man in the city. His headphones played soft music before it was interrupted by a static-ridden voice coming through the other earpiece. He had a FM receiver wired to one ear while the radio still went to the other.

"They're discussing money upstairs," the voice in his earpiece reported. "Just as Nova predicted, they're spending too fast. It looks like you're going to get a chance at some of

Shoeghit's illegal slush fund money like you'd hoped. They're arguing about it now." Steve's head didn't move, he kept labeling envelopes without as much as a flinch. "Should we send in Touw for deep penetration?" the voice in the headphones asked.

Steve finally broke from his routine, reaching to his belt and keying the mike twice on the cassette player.

The voice came back on his headphones, "10 4, receive an affirmative, verify affirmative, that is green light: go ahead."

"Click, Click," Steve keyed the mike twice again.

"10-4, Touw's got the go ahead."

Steve looked up, eyeing a table of women on the other side of the room sitting around chatting as they work. Dressed professionally in a business suit sitting with a lawyer and two real estate brokers was Nova, giggling and chatting, passing time in conversations. Each was half-heartedly doing the work, more concerned with being seen helping out than actually doing so. Nova, whose real name was Nora, looked over in a casual glance making eye contact with Steve and then refocused her attention on the ambitious group. She had an earpiece hidden under her long black hair with a skin-colored wire running down the back of her jacket. That was all the signal Steve needed to understand she got the message.

Twelve noon. Most the volunteers had left for lunch with only a few remaining to work on through the noon hour. Steve remained working, listening to the soft music and getting up to grab a doughnut once in awhile from the coffee stand. Nova removed herself to a supposed lunch—actually running in her heals two blocks to their forward command post in a hotel room they had rented and stuffed with equipment they might need.

An Asian gentleman walked through the main entrance at the campaign and approached the receptionist. His expensive suit and jewelry made it clear he was no volunteer.

"Hello. Welcome to the Frank Ross For Mayor Campaign. May I help you?" She said, looking up from her magazine she was reading.

"Yes. I have a contribution to drop off."

"Wonderful! I can take it here. Do you need a receipt?"

"No, I would like to give it to Mr. Ross in person."

"Do you have an appointment?"

"No, but I'm not just going to give four-thousand dollars anonymously. I suppose I could make an appointment."

"Oh... so you have multiple contributions?"

"No, just from myself. Although if candidate Ross could assure our import-export company that he will stick to his reapportionment policy he's described, my other partners would gladly donate more."

"Yes sir, I understand. Are you aware that the city imposes a five hundred dollar limit on donations?"

"No, I wasn't....Well... I suppose my money's not needed on that account. Thank you for your time."

"Um! Sir!.. Please wait one minute." The receptionist lunged out of her seat showing concern, "Let me get someone down here that can help you who is more familiar with finances than I am."

Touw smiled politely and sat down in the couch placed alongside the entrance door.

The receptionist dialed upstairs and whispered into the phone for a good minute then hung up and smiled again. "Sir, someone will be right with you."

Almost instantly the political consultant

appeared at the top of the stairs coming down quickly. Walking right past all the volunteers as if they weren't there, Jack went straight to Touw.

"Hello! How are you? I'm Jack Swanson. I'm in charge of the campaign. Please come on upstairs where we can have some privacy." The two men walked up the stairs, "And your name, sir?"

"David, David Tran."

"I apologize for the confusion. Everyone's at lunch and we've been just swamped these last couple days."

At the top of the stairs they went to Jack's office directly opposite Frank's.

Touw sat down with a degree of sophistication Jack noticed. Good posture, confidant, waiting for Jack to speak before he did. This was how the old money aristocrats from the East carried themselves. Jack had done his homework.

"So I hear you weren't aware of the stupid limitations we have to abide by."

"No."

"Sir, we greatly appreciate the money and need all the financial assistance we can get. The whole election hinges on getting the message out there." He paused for a second for effect. "If the public can't hear what we have to offer the people of this wonderful city, we're going to come up short. The polls have us neck and neck. It's imperative we get our message out."

"I understand," Touw responded. "The reason I'm here is because of your stand on reapportionment. Our import business needs that to remain the same. If this incumbent gets his way he'll squeeze us for another million in taxes and cut those real estate people that back him another fat tax break like he did when he won the first time. We're sick of this shit, if I may speak candidly. He's squeezed the minorities too far this time. We're tired of paying for his friends' tax breaks. We need a new man in the mayor's office, one that's more responsive to our needs. Five hundred, even five thousand dollars is peanuts compared to what we'll lose if the incumbent wins. I'm not alone in my opinion on these pricks either. I have the Asian-American community fully behind me."

Jack was a little surprised at Touw's knowledge of American slang. "I see. Well... We need all the money we can get our hands on..."

"And also, I want to meet this guy. I want to see if he is sincere in person."

Jack interrupted, "He's in his office now. Please understand he's very busy. We're preparing for a very important rally this afternoon at three thirty. It's imperative this rally goes well with the primary less than a week away."

"I understand, but our corporation's backing isn't unconditional and I want to meet him face to face, so after the election when he's mayor he'll recognize who paid the rent."

Jack leaned back in his chair, and thought for a minute.

Touw stared at him, concerned. "I'm fully aware of how the American political system works. Our attentions are normally focused on senators and governors in the import business. If you and this Frank Ross have any aspirations of a future beyond city politics, you better learn to appease everybody."

Jack didn't hesitate. Without saying a word he got up and motioned Touw to follow him to the other office. Knocking on the door firmly, "Frank, I have someone important I would like you to meet." He tried the handle, peeking in, and then entered. Frank stood up from behind his desk extending a hand to shake as Touw crossed the room to meet him. Jack sat himself in one of the two chairs facing Frank's desk, not adding anything, realizing that Frank was quick enough to know that if someone could get invited in to see him at this crucial time in the day, he must have something substantial to talk about.

"Frank Ross. Pleasure to meet you."

"Hello. David Tran." Touw sat down after shaking hands. "I came down to support to the campaign, but I was unaware that the smaller city political scenes set limits to the amount you can donate."

"It makes it difficult to raise the money we need," Frank said, keeping his comments short to speed along the conversation.

"I'm not going to tie you up today with our issues, or shall we say interests, we're committed to," Touw took control of the conversation, "but while I'm here let me write you a check for five hundred dollars. I was going to give you cash, four thousand to be exact, but I'll go back and have the other concerned parties write you multiple checks for five hundred each. I assume you can take cash, right? After all, eight people gave me five hundred each for you to use for advertising, or whatever you need it for.

That would be legal right?"

"Yes, yes it definitely is." Jack interjected. "The only thing is, in all the commotion, our office supplies have dwindled and we're out of receipts."

"Not a concern, as long as your memory is good. Frank. Jack. Remember who your friends are."

Frank nodded his head staring at Touw.

Touw pulled out a role of money with a gold clip on it and handed it to Jack. "Now I have your attention," he said confidently, self-composed. "How much do you need?"

"Twenty-five times that by five o'clock and I'll make sure you have my cellular phone number when I'm the mayor. I'll be accessible to you twenty-four hours a day, three hundred sixty five days a year."

"I can do that... But not by five."

"Damn! Oh, I'm not upset at you, Mr. Tran," Jack said, "Yes, we'll need that for the final election after the primary. How soon can you get it to us?"

"Two, maybe three days."

Jack got up and walked to the closet at the side of the door, and opened it. He squatted down to his knees and pulled a shopping bag out from the bottom, exposing a safe.

"We will be seeing a lot of each other," Frank started in.

Ignoring him, Touw watched over his shoulder as Jack dialed the combination to the safe in the bottom of the closet located under a stack of files, opened it, and tossed in the money. After the door was open, he looked back, "Ah yes, I look forward to a long healthy relationship. In business and as friends. And hopefully a long productive political career to support you along. All of our candidates we back seem to do quite well. I wonder why that is?" Touw smiled mischievously. "I guess that's all I need to talk to you about." He stood up and extended his hand. "We'll call ahead when we come down with the larger sum. We'll need to take some security precautions. You have security, right?"

"Um," Frank paused, "Yes, of course, kinda like in the Vegas casinos: you can't see the security but it's there."

Touw laughed, "Yeah, like Vegas all right, I walk in with money, and walk out without it. I won't keep you any longer." He exchanged handshakes again. "You will get a call when I come down in a couple days. I'll see myself out, gentlemen." Touw walked out not wasting any time or making conversation with anyone.

"Call Bill now!" Frank bellowed out. "Better than that I'll call him myself. Leave me alone. I need some privacy. Call the station and confirm with them we'll have the money tonight."

Jack took off out the door, while Frank dialed up his main financial backer. "Bill, I need that two hundred K you offered now. Can you do it...?"

Touw was half out of his suit, already in his T shirt as he entered the hotel room two blocks away from the target. He bumped shoulders with Nova as she was leaving to return from her lunch. "You hear?"

"Most of it," Nova replied, pausing for a moment. "Terrence said they made the call for the money the minute you left, and it's supposed to be there about two or two-thirty. A lady named Elena is the courier. Two bodyguards. I'm curious. Where did you put the bug, Touw?"

"In the garbage can. It will go out with the trash tomorrow, in case they have security sweep the place after the primary."

"Good, I must go. Call Terrence. He's waiting."

Touw pulled his slacks off, exposing his boxer shorts with martini glasses on them, then shut the door behind Nova. He dialed Terrence at base. "Yo, it's Touw."

"Good job babe, we have a green light for the snatch. The combo?"

"First, number 10 give or take one or two digits. A turn and a third to the right, and three quarters back." Touw rubbed his forehead. "That's the best I could do."

"That should be enough. Steve just needs you to get him in the ball park. He could crack it without any help, but with that information you just cut twenty minutes off the amount of time it will take."

Two-thirty: The small army of volunteers had returned from their lunch and were sitting down at their tables and refocused on the tasks given them. Nova sat relaxedly working with her three new friends, chatting like retirees in a quilting circle. Steve played the part of the eccentric recluse, sitting by himself at the end of the long coffee table with his headphones on, working away. His attention was not on the matters at hand while he listened to Terrence talking in the earpiece, alerting him that candidate Frank Ross upstairs had just received a phone call that the courier Elena and her two bodyguards had left with cash ten minutes ago and should be arriving anytime now.

The door opened from the garage area. Steve immediately spotted the mark. Elena was an older lady in a conservative business suit with a satchel-style purse slung under her arm. She had long blond hair graying slightly in spots and pasty skin on her roundish face. Hints of her younger day's beauty still stayed with her. He smiled, "I like this gal. She fits the part," he mused as watched her walk in ignoring the people like they were peasants and proceeding straight upstairs, with her two goons right behind her. "I won't find myself feeling sorry after this job," he mused looking back down at his envelopes in front of him.

"Click, click."

"10-4, copy, the guest has arrived." Terrence's voice came back into their headphones.

Their theatrics could use a little work, Steve thought to himself: an old lady with two football player types trying to smile disarmingly, passing this off as something you would see every day. Yeah right!

Nova looked up at Steve and excused herself from her circle of addressers at her table, then proceeded to the one restroom on the lower floor.

Watching his wristwatch Steve counted three minutes, then pushed his chair back stood up, and stretched exaggeratedly. He extended his arms straight up, his shirt tail popped out of where it was tucked into his pants. He left it hanging out for effect, as he walked over to the restroom door. He tried the handle—it's locked, with Nova on the other side holding it to be sure. He paced back and forth showing his need to use the facility, and knocked on the door repeatedly. No response. Another lady lined up behind Steve looking at him inquisitively.

"I hate co-ed bathrooms," he said loudly. "Damn women take all day." The lady behind him was not amused.

Diane jumped up from one of the tables in a rush to try to defuse a potential problem.

Steve grabbed his genital area like a kid would to stop an accident. "Come on! Come on damn it!"

People in the room, aware of what was going on, curiously refrained from looking, up not wanting to add to the embarrassing predicament the two ladies were in.

Diane gently touched him on the shoulder, "Why don't you use the one up stairs just this once. They won't mind, up the stairs and to the right. If anyone stops you, tell them I said it is OK."

Steve didn't respond to Diane, but snapped his head away and went upstairs hurriedly, not looking back. Diane watched him disappear upstairs and then smiled politely at the lady waiting. "I'm sorry, some of our volunteers' social skills aren't the best. He is one of our best workers however, so we try to be understanding." The lady smiled and nodded, placating Diane.

At the top of the stairs Steve quickly looked around. The courier and her security were nowhere to be seen among the workers. This could only mean that they had gone into the main office. Terrence would have an ear on their conversation. Time to disappear. Steve entered the restroom on the second floor.

At the headquarters located in a cheap apartment in the tenderloin of downtown SF, Terrence listened in on the conversation on one of the banks of scanners set up. "Base two Touw, are you in position?"

"10-4, ready."

"Steve, Touw's ready, you've got the go ahead."

"Click, click."

Terrence leaned back in his chair massaging his ear under his headset, "That's it, now we wait. I just hope we don't have to use Touw to jack the place if Steve gets caught. On the jack or on the prowl I guess it doesn't matter. One way or another we'll have our money tonight and I'm on vacation." Terrence opened a tab on top of a soda and took a sip.

Three o'clock: the doors opened to Frank's office and the group of political players emerged hurriedly telling people to get to the rally. Frank Ross and Jack Swanson rushed down the stairs while putting on their coats and snugging up their ties. Elena and her security lagged behind apparently not going to the rally, protecting the carefully structured image of their candidate. The rest of the paid staff drained out behind them as if the room had been flushed like a toilet, leaving only one worker to answer the phones upstairs and a receptionist. The lone worker relieved at having some privacy, lazily pecked at his computer watching the clock constantly. Downstairs Nova purposely saw herself out last. Only Diane stayed longer insuring everyone had rides.

"Click, click, click." She keyed her mike hidden in her jacket as she went to her car.

"10-4, Nova."

"Show time, repeat show time," Terrence whispered into his microphone."

Steve returned the two clicks and crawled down out of the artificial ceiling. Gently he eased himself onto the lid of the toilet and peeked out of the stall. Outside the restroom he heard the phone ring. The lone worker answered. He explained politely that the calling party would have to call again later when the workers had returned from the rally.

Grabbing the door at the bottom with the tips of his fingers Steve pulled it open. The phone rang again and was answered leisurely by the single worker. Crawling like a marine under barbed wire, Steve started across the floor using the desks for cover. The unusually loud voice on the phone could be heard across the entire room. The worker tried to encourage the man to call back but the loud voice on the phone kept talking to him asking questions. It was a good diversion. Terrence could keep that guy talking for hours.

After crossing the length of the second floor Steve held up at the door to Frank

Ross's office, peering back over the tops of the desks at the worker insuring he wasn't looking. He reached into the chest pocket of his thermal shirt and pulled out a glass vial with a rubber stopper in the end of it. Only taking his eyes off the worker talking on the phone for a second he uncorked the vial and carefully poured the liquid onto the neck of the aluminum door handle. The knob fell off. His hand caught it with perfect timing as he'd done on more than one occasion.

He reached into his chest pocket again and produced a small screwdriver, one of the types you get in a give-away with a tiny magnet on the end and a clip on it like a ball point pen. Quietly he probed it into the melted off area of the lock and twisted the mechanism, releasing the latch and opening the door. Ever so slowly he inched the door open avoiding any chance of the hinges creaking. Just enough space existed for him to slip in.

After painstakingly squeezing through, he looked out one more time and then shut the door. Standing up casually now, he inspected the room while putting on some gloves he had removed from his front pants pocket. Stroking and twirling his beard as he thought under pressure, he reminded himself that this was what kept him young. He was the oldest of the master thieves, the real mayor of the city, able to solve any problem anywhere any time. Once in a while he had to earn his keep, and today his dues were due.

A quick look around the room for any visible signs of alarms Touw might have overlooked. Nothing. He walked to the closet running his fingers along the edges of the door feeling for any abnormalities. Eyeing the closet carefully, he reached down and keyed the mike on his cassette player, "I'm in." A four-second pause of complete silence before Terrence came back through his headphones, "10-4... What's the call? Burn it, blow it, crack it, take it?" Steve heard him but paused before responding. He opened the doors to the closet and inspected the safe nestled in the bottom of it. With his hand on the corner he jerked it some to see if it had been bolted down. It didn't move.

"Crack it," Steve said confidently. "About five minutes."

"You have ten," Terrence responded, "otherwise Touw goes in and we carry it out. Touw, set yourself right in front and be on lookout." Touw pulled the Volvo out into traffic without responding, driving up to the front doors and double parking just back far enough from the entrance not to be observed.

Seven blocks away at the sanitation workers' union hall, Candidate Frank Ross screamed his inspiring enthusiastic speech through the deafening microphones at his adoring supporters. "And I promise the people of this great city of San Francisco, that when I'm mayor, there will be reform in this city on a grand scale. I will bring a new, citizen-sensitive administration! And it will listen to the working men and women! It will respect the laborer! You will be represented!... I promise to expand the door to the mayor's office, open it wide... make it large and open... so the people of this city can walk in to see the mayor, and the politicians can walk out!"

The crowd erupted in cheers. A sea of Frank Ross signs bobbed up and down, side to side. The chant started, "Frank Ross for Mayor! Frank Ross for Mayor!"

In the orchestrated confusion of the crowd, Nova slipped out of the hall to the mezzanine just outside and called in to home base on her cell phone, cupping her other ear to block the noise.

At the campaign headquarters Steve removed the large, early eighties vintage cassette player from his belt and set it on the floor close to the safe. Terrence had gutted it out last week and replaced the inner workings with a tiny late nineties two-way radio, an FM receiver, and a very sensitive contact mike. Steve unraveled the mike and licked the small rubber suction cup on it, then stuck it to the safe door just above the combination dial, wiggling his finger and cracking his knuckles gently before grabbing the dial.

Confidently he started manipulating it back and forth to gage the resistance of the tumblers. He focused his total attention on his senses of touch and hearing. Listening and feeling for the tumblers to set in alignment, the tips of his fingers spun it back and forth precisely. With Touw's help from earlier he had the first two tumblers by the second attempt. Four more tries but no third number. "Fuck!" He cussed at himself. Steve took a second, breathing normally, arching his back and standing up from the kneeling position. In the top of the closet he spotted a bottle of single-malt scotch stored away for entertaining or maybe a victory celebration. "Well looky here." Grabbing it and spinning the cap off Steve took a big gulp, cringing as it burned down his throat.

"What the status?" Terrence called in.

Steve stroked his beard as he was thinking, "Nothing like a strong shot of scotch to give you a little kick in the ass." He set the bottle down at his side and sat down cross-legged in front of the safe. He read, adjusting his headphones.

"I take it that's a negative," Terrence asserted.

Steve ignored the comment, refocusing on the task at hand. Like a computer he reverted to the unstoppable method. If you got the first two digits and the last is your hitch run the thirty five possible combos for the last number. One handed he started in, 23-18-35 no. 23-18-34 no. 23-18-33...crack! "Still got it, Stud!" The safe door swung open, literally spilling out money. Standing up he grabbed a cloth draw-string bag tucked into the small of his back and started scooping the money into it. Two manila envelopes were also part of the safe's bounty. He stuffed them in the bag as well for interesting reading later. "Hey I feel like Santa, Ho, Ho, Ho, you know," hoisting the stuffed bag over his shoulder. One last thing he thought to himself, kneeling down and grabbing the scotch bottle. He took two huge victory gulps and then poured the remainder of the alcohol on Frank Ross's desk top. "There you go buddy. That ought to burn your ass."

Briskly straight out the door the master thief walked, taking four bounding steps at the lone worker on the second floor.

"HEY, LOOK SHARP!" Steve yelled.

The startled man sitting at his computer swung around in his chair. Steve removed his key chain's pepper spray and sprayed it less than an inch from his eyes, giving him a full dose. The stunned worker shielded his face with his hand as he gagged and fell to the carpet, gasping for fresh air.

Steve spun away euphorically jogging down the stairs with the sack over his shoulder. The receptionist looked at him puzzled as he appeared at the bottom of the stairs. "What?... Someone has to do Frank's laundry," he said at her as he walked out.

She saw him out the door but did nothing.

Touw reached across and opened the passenger door to the Volvo and it fell open scraping the sidewalk.

Steve hurled the bag over the seat into the back and got in, pulling the door in a little before sitting to avoid damaging the new car any more. He looked back at the entrance, but the receptionist was not aware of what had just transpired. He laughed as Touw pulled into traffic calmly like nothing happened. "I hate to use cliché's, but, it was like taking candy from a baby."

Touw smiled his boyish grin, not taking his eyes off traffic. He grabbed the hand-set to the car radio, "Terrence, we're clear."

"Got it, if you need me. Call land line."

"10-4," Touw latched the mike back on the bottom of the dash. "Did my campaign donation incur interest? There are strings attached to my contribution you know. I expect servitude."

Steve chuckled, his penetrating blue eyes showing a humorous glint in the dim light. He turned the heater on to remove the chill of the early winter night air. "Well," stroking his beard, "let's just say Santa hasn't been keeping track of who's been naughty or nice. You'll be spending Christmas in the Bahamas."

******

Back at Frank Ross's headquarters the exuberant staff and volunteers filed back in from the rally soon followed by the candidate, his political consultant, and the media. The different channels set up their cameras on the bottom floor for their live post rally interview for the five o'clock news. Jimmy Lanier, talking on the cell phone, looked inquiringly at Jack Swanson, who was talking to the receptionist. He smiled calmly and held up one finger to Jimmy indicating he needed a minute, then darted upstairs.

Frank Ross, chatting with some people, gave a smile to his supporters as he removed his trench coat and draped it over a chair.

The four different news cameras had their tripods in place. Frank took his position in front of the cameras, Diane fixed his collar.

Jack came down the stairs in disbelief. He quickly composed himself, but Frank could tell something wasn't right. "Go ahead," Jack coaxed them on.

The bright lights came on, the interview ran the gamut of questions. The entire time Jack Swanson was heatedly interrogating the receptionist off to the side of the cameras. "Why the fuck didn't you call?" he said, enraged.

"You don't have your phone on you."

"Did you call the police?"

"No. I wasn't sure if that was a good idea."

Jack thought for a minute looking at the ceiling. "No, don't call. Who was upstairs?"

"That political science student, Phil. He ran off. I think he's afraid you might think he did it."

"God help him if he did," Jack said, "Find him...or never mind, I'll find him. No one's to know...anything. This could throw the election off track."

The spot lights went off. The different news channels started packing up their gear.

Jack approached Channel 6's anchor Jimmy Lanier. "Uh... Jimmy... We need some more time..."

2

"Why aren't you helping us Phil?" Jack Swanson asked calmly in the dim lit room at the back of the sanitation workers' union hall. The two sat across from each other at either end of the long table. A ceiling fan spun slowly moving the stagnant air around in the little-used space.

"I told you I don't know anything."

"You were the only one upstairs when it happened. You must of seen something." Jack paused for an answer but Phil didn't respond, "Is all this information on your resume true? Political Science major at SF State? It better be, because we're checking it out right now, sport. In fact, since you have nothing to hide, I would like you to take a polygraph. Right now."

"Right now?" Phil seemed surprised.

"Right now." Jack paused for a minute, staring at the nervous kid. "Why do you care? You said you didn't see anything."

"I tell you, some guy yelled, and I turned around, and he sprayed mace in my face. That's all I know."

"Well then you won't mind the polygraph. Just to placate us." A gentleman in a light gray suit, short brown hair parted on the side, walked into the room and started undoing a lie detector from the case it was contained in on the far corner of the table beside Jack Swanson.

"Hey, relax kid." Jack reached into the inside pocket of his suit and removed a pack of cigarettes, shaking it 'tilone stuck out, grabbing it with his lips, and then putting it back. The second man looked as if he was almost ready to get started as he extended a power cord out of the box its full length to the wall outlet. Jack lit his cigarette, "So kid, is this what they teach you at school in the books?" He chuckled a bit. This is the part they leave out of the classroom exercises I suppose. So what do you think?" Jack smiled. The man in the gray suit nodded, indicating he was ready. Then he turned and slowly approached his subject.

"About politics?"

"Yeah, about politics."

Phil looked down at the table just in front of himself fumbling with his hands just below the tabletop. "Let me tell you what I know about politics. It's very, DANGEROUS!" Boom! Boom! Phil, holding a snub nose .38 pistol he had removed from his waist minutes earlier, fired off two rounds into Jack Swanson's belly jerking him back, tipping him and the chair over. He jumped up flipping the table on its side. The polygraph crashed to the floor. The interrogator in the gray suit panicked and ran for the door, but

Phil sent the three remaining bullets mercilessly into his back. He fell to his knees and then to his face, blood seeping out of him.

Phil stepped up to Jack Swanson, who was laying in a pool of his blood on his side holding his guts from spilling out. He reached down, picking up the cigarette from beside him that Jack had dropped when shot and took a long deep drag off of it. Bending over at the waist to get within whispering distance of Jack's ear he blew the smoke out into his face. "Well Jack, did I satisfactorily answer your question?"

******

Broadway Street. The old red light district of San Francisco. Before the Loma Prieta Earthquake of '89 the freeway across the Bay Bridge's last exit was onto this point in the boulevard. For forty years it was packed with strip joints and prostitutes. Now it was one of the only lingering casualties of the long gone earthquake. Most of the red light operations had moved to more accessible areas, only a couple remained. An area of the city in limbo, the city that itself resembled the land-starved, overcrowded New York. Precious space so desperately needed. Trendy new yuppie-oriented North Beach style eateries with their nouvelle cuisine were starting to pop up, spilling over from Columbus Street in this area. An odd mix alongside the neon signs with ten-foot tall nude women on them. A smattering of the old-style Chinese greasy spoons squeezed into every leftover inch of space not already spoken for, as Chinatown's massive girth from across upper Broadway simply forced its way into the area like the unstoppable sand dunes of the desert.

Steve enjoyed coming down here when he was restless. The streets were alive with energy like a hive. Young, old, rich, poor: it was all here. All levels of society circulated in and out of all the alcoves, interacting with each other in their own ways. Everyone fit in. His idea of a utopian society, or at least as close as this world would ever get to one.

The cool night air had become humid and started to drizzle erratically. Steve snugged up his blue windbreaker as he dodged through the endless crowds on the sidewalks. Stuffing his hands into the bottom of his pockets, he stopped only momentarily at a news vender to grab a paper. The skies opened up with a steady downpour. Quickly he jogged down two doors and entered one of the many noodle houses. The bright fluorescent light and stark decorations suited him fine. He had a fondness for the simple honesty of diners and noodle houses. The charades of the trendy places irritated him. Good food, and a lot of it. Not a tease of a taste and a large bill like the five star eateries specialized in. Only a local big-city night rat like Steve could revel in its simplicity among the sophistication-blinded looking for the perfect restaurant to compliment their tailored images.

He pulled back a chair, the steel legs making a shrill noise on the linoleum floor. The small restaurant had six tables stuffed into a space better suited for five. Soft green walls with unframed, tacked-up posters of Asian girls holding up different beer brands. One counter with a sneeze guard separated the grill directly behind it. A wall behind the grill separated the restroom and storage. That was the whole restaurant. You wouldn't find any tourists in here.

Steve pulled a menu out from where it was stuffed between the hot-sauce and ketchup in the middle of the table. The ancient Chinese man behind the counter in his heavily stained apron simply looked over to him. "Won Ton soup, twice cooked pork and a beer," Steve said from across the empty room.

The old man acknowledged by nodding his head and turned to begin cooking. A little kid barely visible above the counter went to the clear glass cooler against the wall in the back and removed a bottle of beer, opened it, and set it at his table, along with an empty glass. Steve pondered to himself, "You see old boy, this place has sophistication. You got a glass for your beer." A dusty old television set on the top of the cooler had the evening news on.

"More updates on the breaking developments in the Frank Ross mayoral campaign."

Steve relaxed in his chair, "I don't believe it," he thought to himself, "They reported the break-in. How fucking stupid. You can't claim that money. It will cost you votes. I thought you guys were sharper than that."

"As reported earlier, Frank Ross's campaign manager Jack Swanson was found with two gunshot wounds to his stomach and is in critical condition in the intensive care ward at SF General Hospital. A senior union official was killed in the same shooting in the parking lot of the sanitation workers' union hall, whose identity is being withheld pending notification of next of kin. Police have no motive or suspects for the shooting. An investigation is in progress at this time. Frank Ross issued only a brief statement saying, quote 'I am completely overcome emotionally by the tragic events. Our prayers are with Jack, and with the friends and family of the slain Union official, and we will do whatever we can to bring thefull weight of justice down on the murderer.' Frank Ross's incumbent opponent Mayor Larry Bennard said that, quote, 'I was

shocked and stunned at the turn of events,'
offering his prayers and any help needed from
the mayor's office.

"One can only wonder if this a sign of
things to come for the reform platform of the
Ross campaign, fighting to take back the city
from corruption. Will he give in to the violence
or keep on campaigning the next two pivotal
days to the primary? Jimmy Lanier, Channel 6
News."

The news continued on, but Steve was
transfixed by what the report had said. It hit him
hard. "I got a bad feeling about this." He
meditated on the situation. It didn't make sense
for either side. I would rule out Mayor Bennard.
The last thing he needs is for someone to get
killed on practically the eve of the primary. No
way in hell he would authorize a hit on the
opponent. Especially now. It plays right into
Frank's hands. Bill Shoeghit might've thought
Jack arranged the safe job, but he could've taken
care of that situation after the fact. He wouldn't
jeopardize the election. Although, in a win he has
to pay the sizable bonus to that jerk. Kill Jack
Swanson, get out of the million-dollar bonus and
slant the election? Possibly. Plus eliminate one
suspect in the missing campaign money
situation? No, no, couldn't be. 1The former
Israeli army type hit man Shoeghit usually had

with him, wouldn't pump two bullets into Jack's belly and walk off. Jack's head would've looked like Swiss cheese. What the fuck is going on here? Steve massaged his forehead thinking.

The old man handed off the food to the kid, who walked it over to Steve. He smiled as the kid handed him his steaming hot plate piled high with food.

"Thank you."

"Would you care for a fork sir?"

"Oh, no thanks, I'll try my luck with the chop sticks."

The kid went back to his spot behind the counter.

Steve opened the slightly wet newspaper, which seemed to have lost its appeal after the news on the television. He put it down, gazing out the window, slowly eating his meal. A group of attractive girls walked by dressed in the uniforms of whores, distracting him from his thoughts momentarily. Skin tight dresses and spiked heels. Probably off to work at one of the remaining strip clubs. A couple of men in suits walked into the restaurant guardedly looking the place over. Steve looked them over carefully but made sure not to make eye contact. Their hard faces didn't match the businessman outward appearance. The first man looked at the cook and then looked at Steve who returned his own gaze to the pork plate in front of him. To his surprise the man walked up. Steve paid him no mind.

"You eat like a pig." He said pointedly to Steve.

Steve peered up from his dinner. The stare from the squinty-eyed and flat-nosed man seemed uncalled for. The man accompanying him walked behind Steve, but Steve quickly shifted in his chair putting his back to the wall.

"Do you mind? Fellas, this is my dinner I'm trying to enjoy here."

"Dinner can wait."

Steve looked at them, puzzled.

"Your presence," the second goon said, "is requested with an associate of ours." Their stares follow him unwaveringly.

"This must be some mistake. You have me confused for someone else."

"No we don't, thief!" The hard stare from the first goon was unwavering. His squinty eyes were ready to draw blood.

"I suppose I couldn't get it to go?"

To Steve's surprise a Lincoln town-car was waiting outside expecting them as they left. No one knew he was down here; he was a bit rattled. The three men got in the back together, Steve being the lunchmeat in the sandwich. They seemed practiced at this process, almost nonchalant. That really made Steve's anxieties rise. The driver, impeccably dressed in a suit, throttled the car into traffic immediately upon the rear door shutting.

"Whatever this is guys, you got the wrong man."

"My employer says you're a thief," Squinty Eyes challenged.

"Tell him he's wrong," Steve replied firmly.

"You'll have a chance to do that yourself. I want you to tell Bill Shoeghit he's wrong. Just maybe he'll believe you. Just maybe he won't."

The car pulled up at the third of the four Embarcadero Towers five blocks from Broadway and entered the garage in the basement. It drove to the elevator doors, not parking, and Steve was ushered out into the elevator by his two captors. It was the thirty-fifth floor before the doors opened to the nondescript hallway. Small scuffs on the off-white walls and dingy matted-down carpet were signs of a busy day life on this floor. For some reason Steve wasn't scared as they walked down the empty corridors to a door propped open at the end of the hall. He felt calm, enjoying the intensity of the moment. This was one of his gifts in life, he could always think well under extreme pressure.

They entered the small space, a partially

renovated forty-by-forty area. Wiring hung down from the panels to the drop ceiling. Boxes and office furniture were strewn about. Some chairs and a desk in the very corner were the only furnishing properly placed. The rain came down hard now outside and pattered at the large windows. The sealed skyscraper however prevented any stimulation from the cleansed air or invigorating brisk chill of the water falling out of the sky. A helicopter flew between the towers purring out through the city's skyline. Steve imagined himself in his helicopter, the love of flying was the bug that had bitten him.

"Beautiful isn't it?" A voice came from behind the aluminum struts of a partially finished wall.

Being stubborn about playing along, Steve sat down in one of the chairs without permission. He didn't remove his gaze from the skyline outside the windows. "Small talk. OK. Beautiful city skyline as seen from ripped-to-shreds office while being held captive by a couple of violent Israeli thugs. OK, I'll play. Yes it's beautiful."

An older, heavy-set Jewish man, gray hair on the side, bald on top, thin-rimmed glasses, walked over and sat in the chair next to Steve. His two roughneck men took seats, one behind the desk and the other in the last empty chair to the right of Steve. "You're not being held captive, smart guy. If I decide that I want you held, there will be no gray area in that matter."

"Shoeghit, what do you want?" Steve says pointedly.

"You know the problem with males? You can't get their attention unless you got them by the balls... You won't listen to me unless I cause you pain. I've learned that through the years," Shoeghit leaned forward in his chair into Steve's field of view. "You follow me?"

Finally Steve looked at him, looking more at his nose and mouth than at his eyes. Not giving him the pleasure of the stare-down.

"You think you're so fucking cunning. This is the year 2000 dumb ass. The computers do the thinking. The only thing that gets you places is control. And how do you control men? Pain! Physical and mental."

Steve just sat, unresponsive.

"Don't be an asshole Steve Armstrong! Roddy," Shoeghit nodded and motioned to squinty-eyes. Roddy reached down opening a drawer in the desk and broke out a bottle of expensive Louis XIV Cognac and some large shot glasses, poured four drinks and shoved them at each man. Steve took it, tasting a small sip and then returning to his poker-faced stare at Bill Shoeghit.

"Someone ripped me off for two hundred grand."

"Embarrassing," Steve said unconcerned, taking another sip from the glass.

"No sir, not embarrassing, because I've got the money back and the perpetrators...well...by the balls."

"Congratulations. Is that all? You feel better now that you have that off your chest."

The squinty-eyed roughneck Roddy reached into his inner jacket pocket and pulled out a picture setting it on the table in front of Steve. He looked down. It showed Terrence and Nova tied back-to-back on the floor, at some location unfamiliar to Steve.

"They don't mean anything to me." Steve was bluffing, but he tried to sell that he wasn't.

"That's good. Because we killed them right after we took that photo...I...feel satisfied with my self-administered justice system. It works much better than the proper one. You know... you, you're a rare talent." Shoeghit stretched back in his chair, "You've made it longer than most. I respect endurance. My own endurance is on my mind now, Steve Armstrong. You saw the news. I'm a suspect in a shooting. And what kicks my ass, is—I didn't even do it! A hundred and twenty two murders and I'm going to go down for one I didn't do. That's not fair. Those fucking cops got motive on me too. I had no alibi ready. It happened in the union hall I control.

Can you see my dilemma? And the other main suspect is the mayor, who appoints the police chief in this city. Do you think he's getting investigated? I doubt it. Guess what? I got this feeling I'm going to get fucked. Now you know, and I know, that I'm smarter than the sequence of events that just transpired. But if you're on top of things what's the next logical move for Mayor Bennard?"

Steve stared back not offering any answer.

"Well, the voter support will swing to Frank Ross, a man of impeccable credentials, because he's been violated by the bad guys, i.e., the corrupt Mayor. But then sting the investigation and the polls by saying it was all planned. A set up. And arrest Bill Shoeghit. Whether you can make it stick or not isn't important. By the time the verdict's in the election will be over. They are a cunt hair from having enough to make the warrant. They take me in and Frank Ross is done, washed up in this town. Roddy..." Shoeghit nodded again.

Roddy reached below in the leg space cut out of the desk and pulled out a satchel, tossing it on the desk. "Two hundred grand of well-traveled money. It went from me, to Frank, to you, to me and back to you. You're working for me now, Armstrong. You're going to find out what actually happened."

"And what if I say no?"

"I'll skin you alive. I'll bring one of my doctors in to keep you awake during the whole process. Then we'll cut your hands and feet off and ship you to your mother."

Steve reached out, grabbing the money off the desk top, then stood up to leave. "OK, I got your point. One question. How did you find me?"

Squinty-eyes answered, "You should never hang around the scene of the crime."

Steve looked at him questioningly.

"A radio direction finder pointed to the wire your sweet little girl had hidden in her suit. We followed her to your tenderloin apartment you rented and found the other member of your operation and the money. Never trust people with your money stupid. The security camera at the door gave us a rough idea of what you looked like, and after raping your little girl with a piece of barbed wire wrapped around a wooden dowel, she felt—oh shall we say aroused—to tell us where you hung out. You'll find a phone number in the satchel you can reach me at. Don't call unless you have something good to say."

"How can I be sure you won't kill me?"

Shoeghit stared at him, not answering directly as Steve paused, looking back.

"What's the point in getting you off the hook if I'm dead anyway? You killed my team, my only two friends. What's the point?"

"In this world everyone needs a reason. Money, cause, religion. You're a thief. The best in California. I checked around. Your credentials are impeccable. The two chumps you were working with were no better than car thieves before you taught them. They had no loyalty to you. After this is over I'll play you a tape of them trying to cut a deal to give you up for their freedom. There's no honor among thieves. There's no loyalty in your—what was it called?—Listener Thieves' guild." The three men broke into laughter. "I'm the crime boss in this town. I have a hundred men who will go to jail for me, kill, whatever. Violence is power. Sneaking around and stealing is a pussy's way to commit crimes. My men are my family. And my family better not see their beloved father in jail. You will stay breathing as long as I decide you will. That's your ticket to living, keeping me happy. We'll settle this problem I blame you for by the way, and then we'll discuss your working arrangements."

Steve remained poker faced not showing the inner disgust he was feeling through all his being.

"You claim to have honor in you," Shoeghit exclaimed. "You claim it by having the balls to pretend you're hurt by the loss of your two working partners. You will show your honor by getting me out of the mess you created. Got it, Asshole? Find this Phil tonight. You know, to me you're a phony, no better than the crack addicts sleeping in the gutter. Prove your honor! Prove me wrong or die. Now get the fuck out of my sight."

Steve left, walking quickly out of the room and to the elevator, not looking back. As he entered the elevator and the door shut cutting him off from the floor, he realized that Shoeghit's words had shaken him. He was questioning himself, when he had never thought twice about his motives. He always considered himself to be Robin Hood, stealing from the rich. But there was no giving to the poor. His two friends were dead. He brought them up to the big score level. Elevated them from their petty crimes. The big stakes. Big crimes. And now they paid the big price. His throat was scratchy, his eyes watering up with tears, but then he thought, I wonder if they tried to sell me out or buy some time. They wouldn't do that to me, after all I did for them. I want to see that tape Shoeghit has. I want to see their eyes. The elevator opened to the lobby, Steve darted out into the downtown's busy streets. At least they didn't get Touw, I must contact him immediately and tell him everything. Honor, we'll start there. Let's see if there is honor in Touw's heart.

The night passed at Steve's loft, in a South-of-Market alley. Unable to rest he tried to contact Touw throughout the night. A call to his message machine, a page, and an E-Mail to his computer. No response. He had mentioned slipping off to a short vacation, Steve, remembered, but where and how long was the problem. I didn't expect any problems, Steve mumbled, frustrated with himself. In the darkened room a single buzz from the door intercom interrupted the quiet. Steve, lying on his back on the leather sofa, staring out the large drawn shade into the empty alley, was startled into poise. Who was at his door at four in the morning? He got up, walked over and pressed the intercom. "Yes?" he said deep and gruff.

"It's Roddy, let me up."

"Why? It's not time yet. It's only been a couple hours."

"What the fuck are you talking about? I brought the tape."

Tape? Steve thought for a minute. They're actually going to show me the video of Terrence and Nova getting killed? He buzzed the door, carelessly letting him in. Not really thinking any thoughts he waited for Roddy to come to the top of the steps. Steve didn't know what to think. Didn't have an opinion at this time. But he was sure he wanted to see it. He was intensively sure he wanted to see it. Watching his friends die at the hands of these butchers would fuel his motivations at a later point.

Roddy walked in, the chill of the night air still radiating off his clothes. He handed the tape to Steve, poking it at him.

"Thanks, I guess. Now, may I have some privacy?"

"No, Get your ass over there, turn on the TV and get to work," Roddy ordered him.

"Get to work?"

"Yeah, it's a tape of the Jack Swanson shooting. I can't leave it here, so hurry up and watch it and get what you need off of it."

Steve turned his back to Roddy powering up his components on his TV and VCR quickly. "I guess the police don't have a copy of this."

"Damn right they don't. We're our own police," Roddy proclaimed.

"Wouldn't this get Shoeghit off the hook?"

"The case as it stands right now couldn't get a conviction," Roddy blurted out, "No DNA, gun, etc. Shoeghit's defense team would get him off. You are stupid aren't you? You really believed that speech of panic he gave you 'Oh save me or I'll be framed.' The case is strong enough to get an arrest that's all, which means no mayor Frank Ross, which means, you are fucked. Got it? Spell it a little clearer for you? Lose the election and you would be best to kill yourself, because Shoeghit will slowly peel your skin off, and grind it into sausage right in front of your eyes. That's what he does, I've seen him do it. It's your fault this whole predicament happened. Ross was ahead and sailing along to a win. Not now, it's all fucked up, and the only reason you're alive is he needs your skills to fix things up. Got it?"

"So it still doesn't answer why not give the tape to the police." Steve understood, but he wanted Roddy to keep explaining while he grabbed a second remote using the sleight of hand only a magician or a thief would have and hit record on his second VCR he used for pirating movies he rented. As the infuriated Roddy kept defining the situation he broke eye contact only once to make sure it was dubbing.

"The political consultant, and the union's internal security PI, interrogating a poor political science student about an incident, namely the break-in that you did. He gets squirrelly and caps both of them in Shoeghit's union-halls back room. Exactly what part of that don't you find unusual?" Roddy caught his breath composing himself. "I'm responsible for you now. I'm your liaison to Shoeghit. You deal with me! Got it motherfucker?"

Steve nodded to the question, as the security video began playing. The small room with the three men around the table. He sat quietly watching not worried about picking up any details off the tape yet, because he could watch the copy he was making, later. The only point Roddy affirmed with his tough guy speech was that they're keeping him alive only just long enough to solve the situation they're in. They would never let him walk away from the events after it was over. He knew everything. The money they gave him was like a confusion token. They couldn't sit and hold a gun to his head while he was making moves in the city. Shoeghit was very crafty for a gangster. Most wouldn't think in those terms. He had almost made Steve feel guilty about robbing him. Giving him the money back, 'Oh look at the mess I'm in because of you. Yeah fuckin' right! He's a bloodthirsty killer. He offed my two friends without hesitating. Steve's genius of a criminal mind was going to be put to the test here. Do or die, literally. The first thing he needed to do was to create some time for himself to figure a way out of this mess. Mayor Bennard would be making his move probably within twenty-four hours. He was no doubt working out the details of Shoeghit's arrest right now. The cops most likely were sympathetic to him. We need more confusion.

The bang came out of Steve's surround-sound audio system as Jack Swanson's mid-section wrenched backward flipping him out of the chair in the video.

"You realize," Steve leaned forward in his chair pointing at the screen, "that's no political science major?"

"How's that?"

"When he goes for the kill, he calms down. He is thinking, not panicking. One, two... Boom, Boom. He deliberately shoots both of them. Look carefully at his face, he knows exactly what he's doing."

"So he's a hit-man?"

"No, well maybe, but not a very good at it. This is new to him if he is. His first kill. Notice as he leaves, he should've stopped and put one right through Jack Swanson's temple. But he doesn't. Maybe that's when panic hit. After he took a drag on the cigarette. It's weird. Jack's still alive right?"

"Yes, if you could call it that. They removed most his stomach into a bag. They're going to attempt to find some organs, but he'll never be the same man he was."

"I need to talk to him."

Roddy pulled out a cigarette and lit up in the dim light. "The police tried but he couldn't respond with anything that was logical."

"Anything else to go on?"

"All addresses we had on him were fake. We're trying to get the phone records as fast as we can, but you can bet there won't be anything there if he's a pro."

"I have nothing else to go on but the video...and not even that 'cause you're taking it with you."

"It's your mess... A test to push your skills to the zenith. Embrace this problem like a mathematician would a complex equation." Roddy looked over at Steve slouched down in his chair looking at the screen. "Get some rest." He turned on a lamp on the small table. "Tomorrow at noon you're going over to the mayor's office."

Steve's eyes perked up adjusting to the light and Roddy's comment.

"There's a girl who interviewed with this Phil for a position in the Ross-for-Mayor campaign who was rejected. She has a job fundraising at the Mayor's."

"Are they aware of the connection?"

"Yes, and they don't give a fuck about justice being served. She has security with her twenty-four hours a day since the incident. Makes you wonder doesn't it? We made some threats to get an interview with her. That's the best we could do."

"So you picked me to go?" Steve stroked his beard, thinking. "My ten minutes of fame. That's not the publicity I had in mind."

"You're a thinker, a plotter. You read people. Tomorrow you will represent, or shall we say be the point man, for the second most powerful faction of businessmen in the Bay Area. You will be in the lair of the first. An untempered, calm, thoroughly observant interview is needed. We're the actors. We control through fear and violence. It's not time for that...yet. You need to set the stage for the event."

******

The Lincoln town car smoothly drove up to City Hall, Roddy driving authoritatively into the reserved space in front used for VIPs. Steve felt like he was on display for the whole world to see. Publicity was not a good bedfellow for a thief. He reminded himself that to truly be a master he must be able to move freely in all the realms of society.

Five hardened city official cloned men were at his door as he opened it. "Are you coming?" He quizzed Roddy.

"No, just you. Don't let them fuck with you. Remember who you represent."

Steve didn't respond to him, just got out, slamming the door in disgust. The mistrusting eyes of his escort made him feel jumpy. All five stood there and glared at him for a second to make a point but Steve wasn't going to take any of this bully bull shit.

He shrugged his shoulders, "Well...are we going to do this or what?"

The shortest man of the five, a slightly graying medium-built black man started to talk, "You know you're only here because we allow..."

Again Steve, interrupted, "Am I here to interview you? NO. Take me to the girl now, or tell your boss I left."

Steve enjoyed the power trip. The hushed group now simply walked with him, held in check from the rude behavior his controlled threats would have generated. They took him straight up to the second floor through the mayor's reception area and into a meeting office opposite the actual mayor's quarters. Most of the Saturday staff had gone for lunch but he could feel the tension in the few that were there as they all left and shut the door to the room. Tactics, he mused. They wanted this meeting right in the main office. No funny business here. And of course this whole meeting never happened. God I love to hate these hypocritical jackals. Justice? Ha! A thief playing detective. This makes a lot of sense. He sat down at the small table, savoring the silence.

Five minutes passed before the door cracked

open quietly. In walked a girl. She didn't look like what he had imagined, but he realized she was probably saying the same thing. Uncomfortable in a suit, Steve adjusted the necktie while studying her. About twenty-five, he guessed. Not a drugger or a buzzer, her skin had undefiled, fresh color to it and her eyes were bright green, no trailing tiny red blood vessels in the tear ducts.

"Are you to be my interviewer?" she asked as she walked confidently and stood at the edge of the table. She stood tall and proud, daring Steve to look at her beautiful figure. She wasn't one of those skinny supermodel wannabe spawn trying to excite you with their bony little bodies. Her build was voluptuous, full-figured like Marilyn Monroe, perfectly highlighted by the tight black dress and white blouse with a little black tie. She walked to the window to look out at the haze across the sky.

"Winters in San Francisco are so depressing."

Steve didn't respond.

"What's your name?" She asked, her back still to him.

"Michael."

"It seems you feel I'm involved in some sort of foul play, Michael?"

Steve stroked his beard, thinking carefully how to respond. "I've been requested to do some discovery work on an acquaintance of yours."

"May I ask," She turned and looked at him from the window, "what credentials do you have for this inquiry?"

"Is this to be an interview or an interrogation?" The distinctive, smooth voice of the mayor came from the direction of the doorway.

Turning his head quickly to the other presence, Steve was amazed. There stood the mayor himself. He had seen Mayor Bennard numerous times on television but never in person. He was a very sophisticated, well-polished politician. "Just a few questions. You can call it what you like."

"Would you mind if I sit in? You can understand I have more than a passing interest."

"Not at all. Please have a seat."

The mayor pulled a chair back and sat down. The girl looked noticeably nervous as she walked over to the table and took the end chair.

"Let's start," Steve said. "What's your real name? Keep in mind we can run your fingerprints.

Hesitantly she said softly, "Gena McGrath."

The two men's attention to her every motion and speech inflection was unwavering.

"Who is this Phil, and how do you know him?"

"He goes by Ivan, Ivan the Terrible like the movie. We were going to date but he is too busy with his revolution to spend time with me. I wanted to be with him, that's all, I didn't care about the politics. I went through with the infiltration of the different political factions not because I wanted to destroy them like he did, but because I thought he...loved me." Gena bowed her head.

"His name's Ivan Teranov," Mayor Bennard added, "We did run his prints. He has no police record."

"Has a warrant been issued for his arrest?"

"Do you have some evidence you wish to come forward with to cause that?"

Steve, realizing the complexity and political agendas, withdrew his question by turning back to Gena. "What kind of revolution?"

"Anarchy, order from disorder. The strong shall survive."

"Why did he shoot Jack Swanson?"

"I don't know. It's all supposed to come down. I guess that was the start."

"What's coming down?"

"The corrupt aristocracy that runs this country."

"Interesting," Steve smiled, trying not to let the tone of the conversation become hostile. "I would like to meet with Ivan. How can I find him?"

Gena didn't respond, but shook her head "no."

"Gena," the mayor said, "It would be advantageous for you to tell what you know. This guy, Ivan, he's put you in a lot of trouble. That's not love, honey."

Gena looked a little panicky. "He's a drifter, hard to find. All I know is, he was at the Eden Hotel once when my mother visited me, and he couldn't sleep over. He rented a room for one night. It's a horrible place. I think he went there to make me feel sorry for him. To be sure I didn't change the locks while he was out. You have to understand, he's not a bad person. He's really nice, he'll give you the shirt off his back if you need it."

"Who else is in this group associated with him?" Mayor Bennard asked.

"I don't know. They set it up in cells, like the IRA. You only know the contact person. He was my contact person, that's all I know. I don't want to say any more. No more questions without a lawyer," Gena responded, turning her head away and looking at the blank wall.

The mayor laughed. "You're not under arrest. And besides a lawyer won't save you from the can of worms you opened. You're in deep, Gena. I'll tell you what. You go get that lawyer, OK? But when you get him you have him make you out a will. Got it?"

The room fell silent. Steve looked at both

people. "Who's the criminal here?" he thought to himself. I wonder if this is all an act for my benefit.

"Would you excuse yourself from the room, Gena?" the mayor said pointedly.

She got up and left, her elegant strut replaced by short, worried steps. Walking out the door Gena looked back directly at Steve like she had something more to say, but couldn't. The door shut leaving the mayor of San Francisco and the master thief alone. Politics makes for strange bedfellows, Steve pondered. The person who coined that saying couldn't be more correct.

Mayor Bennard just stared at Steve.

"Thank you for the interview," Steve asserted, attempting to break the uncomfortable silence.

"Is she lying?"

"I don't know."

"Who are you? A consultant? A PI? I know you're not with Ross or Shoeghit."

"I'm just a friend, looking into a touchy situation for them."

The mayor wasn't buying it. "You realize we're not in any way involved with this."

"Of course."

Mayor Bennard leaned forward like he was expecting Steve to add something to it, but he didn't.

"Good day." Steve got up and walked out

leaving the mayor sitting in the room all by himself.

Steve had Roddy take him home after the unnerving meeting with the mayor. A consultant. Not exactly. A thief trying to hunt an anarchist. If that wasn't bad enough, he was working for the machine. The machine that he hated, just like the anarchist. Aristocracy, old money, mob, politicians, pure evil disguised by five hundred-dollar suits and practiced hollow smiles. Helping them out of a bind was against all Steve's principles. Honor. He had stooped to a new level of disgust with himself. Roddy dropped him off. Steve made a list of a couple of things he wanted him to check out before leaving. Once inside his home he darkened his loft pulling all the drapes and played his copy of the video he had secretly dubbed. Steve laid on the floor studying Ivan. "Am I hunting a friend for a foe?" he asked himself, "Shoeghit's right, I have no honor, and I just realized, I have no friends. Self first I guess. Save your own ass at the expense of your enemies.

3

Saturday night 9:00pm. Touw finally called in after catching a news report while stepping off his plane in Hawaii.

"What's happening boss?" Touw's soft voice came across the phone barely discernible through the static.

"Things aren't good."

"Did I leave too early?"

"No," Steve paced the floor of his loft talking on his handheld. "Nothing you could do. Don't tell me where you're at Touw, but just tell me if you brought your passport with you when you left."

"Yes."

"Then Touw, keep going west, understand? Go further west for awhile till things cool off here. Call in once a week to see if I'm still here. If things calm down I'll let you know."

"It's that bad?"

"Our office staff has been cut by half. Not laid off, but terminated."

"I see. If that's the case, let's cut the crap," Touw said. "I'm not running. Expect me in sometime tonight. Set a rendezvous for morning and update me on the situation."

"I don't think that's a good idea, Touw. Your

ingress route to SF will be compromised. I don't think it's wise to come at this time."

"Don't worry about me, I'll contact you tomorrow morning, Steve. Just stay safe and start working up plans to get out of this mess."

"Are you sure you want to do this, Touw? It's not worth it, all of us taking a fall. Bail out now, hide in the homeland for a month or two, then come back. The cash we stashed will still be there, grab it and start a new life."

"No..."

"I'm very concerned that you don't understand the gravity of the situation."

"I don't care. When I get back, just show me the problem. You point, I'll shoot. There's no problem that can't be solved or eliminated. That is all, Steve," Touw's voice was adamant. The receiver clicked off, the dial-tone replacing it.

Things were developing so fast. Steve felt his forehead tensing up like a headache was going to add to his problems. Touw didn't desert the sinking ship. That should help. Now I'm not alone in this. A vote of confidence from my soldier in this battle. Steve walked over to his small kitchen space turning the light on and opening his junk drawer, fumbling through it after aspirins. He found the bottle, opened it, shaking three out into his hand and tossing them into the back of his throat. He reached over to the tap, but then hesitated, "Ah, what the hell, I'll be dead tomorrow anyway." He grabbed the bottle of Glenlivet and washed it down with a big gulp. Slamming his drawer shut, he grabbed his coat off the back of the door and headed out into the city.

Steve realized that he probably had 'til Monday morning to stave off his execution if that was at all possible. The mayor would make his tactically thought-out arrest at sun-up Monday so the rush hour commuters listening to their radios could hear the news that Mayor Bennard wasn't involved with shooting Jack Swanson. If Steve could produce this nut Ivan, a DNA link could be made to him without the use of the incriminating video. And a confession or maybe an ID by Jack Swanson, if his condition improved, would take Shoeghit off the hook and save the election. Or at least that was what Frank Ross and Shoeghit were thinking. The only loose end was himself.

"Why do I feel responsible to these criminals?" Steve quizzed himself with angry frustration. If anyone deserved to be robbed, it's them. I'm lending myself to being their pawn. I should have my head examined. Ivan's more harmless than any of the killers involved. I don't agree with anarchy, but Ivan won't try to kill me after he has what he needs out of me. By noon Monday I'll disappear. Either way it plays out. If

I produce Ivan, then I still know Frank Ross's dirty little secrets, something they won't stand for. On top of that I helped myself to his illegal treasury fund, robbing them. No Ivan to prosecute on Monday, and Mayor Larry Bennard squeezes Shoeghit by forcing an arrest. Frank Ross's main contributor, the power player who arranged for him to use the sanitation workers' union hall with a simple phone call, is locked up for murder. The blame's off the Mayor. Shoeghit's in trouble with a number of motives for the police to use against him.

"Steve, Steve, Steve, what the hell did you get yourself into now?" he scolded himself as he got into his burgundy Audi Q8 in the garage below his loft.

He pulled out into the alley and started on his way to the Eden Hotel. "So what's the plan?" he asked himself as the Saturday night traffic paced along. A thief usually had a number of contingencies set up to cover a gamut of incidents that could arise. For once he was planless, at least for the moment. Steve always argued that the wrong people had the power in this city, maybe now was the time to make the move to wrestle it out of their hands. People don't give up power easily. In ancient times the only way you got power was to pry it from your opponent's dead fingers. "If that's what it takes, so be it! I'm not playing ball for these worthless fuckers. Try to make me a pawn in their little arena. Fuck 'em."

Steve's driving became impatient as his adrenaline raced. He reached over and opened the glove box and pulled out a 9mm Beretta pistol tucking it into his pants in the small of his back.

The Audi pulled into parking across the street from the Eden Hotel. It was an old neglected brick building in the Mission's slummiest area. Home for mostly drug addicts and psychotics. No normal person would stay this deep in the Mission considering there are similarly priced hotels in better parts of the city. The dark rain kept pouring down again, this the third night in a row. The dreary, poorly lit street normally lined with debris in the gutters and on the sidewalks was washed clean by the rains. The Eden almost looked livable except for the hints of its tasteless residents using bed sheets of several different colors as curtains in random windows. Flickering shadows of TVs playing inside a half a dozen rooms showed above the small neon hotel sign. It was a busy night at the Eden. The rain had driven the junkies inside.

Steve crossed the street in a jog, the rain dampening his clothes, and entered through the glass doors. The lobby looked more like the check-in at jail with its steel reinforced doors going past the office and its bulletproof glass. The filthy linoleum floor puddled with water it was unable to absorb causing a stagnant pungent odor.

Calmly Steve approached the window attended by an old man in a brown polyester shirt with a bad toupée uncaringly pulled over his head. His crusty face made him look at least seventy. Steve ran his hands through his hair and beard to get the moisture out of it before he talked to the guy. "Hello," he said into the small silver portal through the glass. "Here to visit Ivan."

"Can't you read? No visitors after ten." The old man pointed at the sign taped at the top of the window. "Besides, he checked out at five." The old man's weathered hand pointed at his vacancy sheet on the desk.

"Did he leave a message when he'll be back?"

"No, he just said check him out and walked off."

"I want to rent his room tonight," Steve said.

The old man looked oddly at him. "His room's not ready. House keeping comes in tomorrow morning. I have two available rooms in the back, no windows. Take it or leave it." The old man coughed after talking, grotesquely spitting out the phlegm into the waste can.

Steve pulled out a hundred-dollar bill and slid

it under the glass. "I'd prefer Ivan's dirty room if you don't mind. The view is better."

After pausing for a second the old man grabbed the hundred. "You're that way huh?" the old guy showed disgust in his raspy voice. He reached under the counter and pushed the buzzer releasing the steel door. Steve pulled it open and stepped through to the back hall and up the stairs. The key to the room slid out a hole between the office and the wall with a little box below it. He grabbed it and proceeded upstairs.

The stench of the hotel seemed to correspond with how high a floor you were on at the moment. Scarred walls patched with sections of tin instead of chalk-board accented the moldy green carpet blackened and rolling up on the sides. The hallway of the third floor was deserted at the moment. Steve hurried to room thirty-nine, quickly opening the door so he could enter and get out of sight.

He paused at the entrance after shutting the door and carefully studied everything. It wasn't too bad inside, Steve thought, bearable. Humid squalid air made it insufferable to his sinuses with the widows shut, but it was cleaner than a normal junkie's room would be. No trash on the floor, counters organized. The bed was unmade and some Styrofoam take-out containers were on the table beside it, but that was nothing unusual.

It didn't seem like a panicked individual resided here. This lent substance to the accusations that Ivan was a militant. Another day on the job for the revolutionary, Steve guessed. It's a lot easier to preach that stuff to your admirers than to actually do it. This guy's for real. He looked so innocent and clean-cut in the video too. Touw and him ought to get together and have a bitch fight. They both look like choir boys on the outside but were predators on the inside.

Steve went to the bathroom first. The third floor was the expensive floor—each room had its own small facility unlike the lower floors where you had to share. You would have to be on drugs to actually use one of them down there, they were so filthy.

******

Steve had a brief stint in the hotels when the CIA booted him in late '98 for not killing a Colombian drug lord. Steve had joined The Company as they call it, to deal drugs which was the main thrust of the operations since the Soviets had disintegrated. The drug lord in question didn't want to play ball and/or obey the United States of America: wear a white-hat rule book of drug dealing. So the CIA decided to take it upon itself to kill him. Steve was pretty sure the President didn't even know what the CIA was doing in South America.

The bosses in The Company only had to hide the illicit money for four years, then a new Commander-in-Chief steps in, oblivious to everything and so on, and so on. He was fired without compensation. Thrown out on the street. The best defense is a good offense, he learned the hard way. The old school agents got that down. Right and wrong are long gone. Someone acts up, doesn't go along with the program, go after him. Destroy him. Make sure he doesn't stay around. His name was purposefully leaked, accusing him of being a DEA spy to the drug cartels. They confiscated his bank account and house, pending an investigation. The only thing they couldn't do was hold him in a cell. They couldn't lose him if they had him detained. They would have to explain things then. The system's last stand. Then they would need a clear reason, not speculation. Steve could have made his little secret public from inside prison.

The powers in The Company put him on the street in downtown L.A. His Levis, shirt, and fifty dollars. Homeless, but not helpless, this was where Steve came into his own. He noticed he had a tail following him. An unmarked car circling plus someone on foot that stood out badly. He found out later why they weren't too worried about whether or not he had spotted them. The Company men were updating his position to a couple of independent hit-men the drug powers had hired. It was a sure thing the CIA was paying for it through one of its well covered slush funds somewhere. They were going to remove the liability to their illicit activities. This wouldn't be the last time Steve had a bounty on his head.

Later that day, Steve spotted these coked-out South Americans a block away packing their cannons under their coats from behind the curtain of the hotel window. They had pumped themselves up so high they were probably going to attack the first person that looked at them cross-eyed. The tail took off obviously wanting to put some distance between them and the ensuing bloodbath. Typical CIA, not worried about who gets hurt in their politics.

This was Steve's chance. It was simple— he had to move. He went to the restroom the floor shared and hid till they walked past. The two men turned the corner and started kicking the door in. Steve went down the stairs, out onto the sidewalk and disappeared into L.A. His ego wasn't helped any by running away, but he was alive.

******

Long hair, a beard, three identity changes, and about twenty burglaries of rich evil undeserving people had transpired between then and now.

Once again a bounty of sorts was on his head. Once again back in a cheap hotel. This time, though, he was the hunter.

The bathroom's small twelve-inch fluorescent light flickered a bit before it came on. Never remodeled in all the years, its fixtures were old. Soft green painted walls stood over pearl white tiling with black triangles in the corner of each individual one. Classic Art Deco.

Steve moved around slowly making no noise. Feeling the room's energy. Looking for answers to his riddle. The old tub was a stand-alone from the fifties. The shower curtain draped inside had moldy mildew working up from the bottom. The tub was so old that the whiteness of the porcelain had worn to clear in some areas from years of use.

Scanning his eyes like a sweeping radar searching the ground, he turned around and sat on the toilet at the end of the tub and thought. The sink basin was porcelain as well, not plastic like most modern ones. It was supported by two thin chrome steel rods. He looked the room over from the sitting perspective of the throne. A thin plastic grocery sack was hanging from the inside handle on the back of the open door to the restroom, barely visible. Steve stood up, walked over and removed it. This Ivan was not a junky. He was relatively certain now. He fell into more of a terrorist category to Steve. He was neat, he put grocery bags on the back of bathroom doors for trash, instead of throwing debris on the floor.

Steve dumped the contents of the sack in the sink. A couple of wads of toilet paper Ivan had used to blow his nose. Some bar napkins, an unopened condom, and a four-inch by four-inch flier for a bar. Big red letters on a purple back ground with white spots all over it, "Blisters." Steve flipped it to the other side, "Blisters, celebrating women in leather every Saturday night. Off Valencia Street at Fourteenth. Twenty-dollar cover no passes. Back room show at ten and midnight." Steve folded it once and stuck it in his pocket.

He walked out to the main room and opened a window to let some air into the stifling space. The room was large with an area for the bed and some space for a sofa. A wooden coat-rack by the door with one rung broken off its top was the only sign of unrepaired vandalism. There was an old oak dresser drawer to the side of the bed in need of a varnish. A plastic table below the TV at the foot of the bed with a green sofa and some standing space to the other side. The room lit by the light from the street beaming in through the windows made creepy shadows off the old furniture as Steve searched the drawers of the dresser. All of them were empty.

Walking over to the nightstand his thin rubber windbreaker's squeaks were noticeable in the silent room. The nightstand had last night's Chinese take-out containers on it. Out of curiosity he picked them each up individually, looking at each one's contents, then throwing them on the floor. He discovered a small note pad and pencil were on the table in between them. Steve picked the little pad up carefully, looking it over. One slip had been torn off the top of the brand new pad. There was no writing on any of the pad though. He reached inside his windbreaker and unbuttoned one of his breast pockets on his shirt and stuck it inside it and re-buttoned it. That's all the story this room has to tell, he acknowledged to himself.

******

Saturday night 9:30 pm Third Street industrial park in South San Francisco. The corner snack shop sold a pack of cigarettes to one last customer, and then the caretaker locked the door behind him as he left, going out to the deserted streets. The rain now was just drizzling but the freezing wind off the bay blew unchallenged down the streets. The gentleman walked on the sidewalk ducking into a recessed doorway of a closed office. Another man waiting back in the shadows greeted him. "Did you get your glorious cigarettes?" he said sarcastically.

His accomplice, unamused, zipped his leather jacket all the way up, "It's fucking freezing in this fucking place, give me a bump." He reached into his front pants' pocket and pulled out a small paper and unfolded it. Ivan leaned against the wall in an attempt to block the wind, pulling out his keys and digging the end of one of them into the paper Dilan cupped in his hand. Ivan put it to his nose and snorted the little lump of powder off the end of it.

"Crack on Brother."

Ivan looked at him irritated, "I wish I had never seen that shit."

"Ah bullshit you love it," Dilan insisted, "It's shown you new worlds."

"No," Ivan replied, "It's blinded me to its energy, and robbed me of a future. A life not dependent on finding energy, besides my own."

"It's liberated you from the trappings of the charade." Dilan argued back, "How many days straight have you been up? Two? Three? Look at all the life you've gained. Sleep is for the slaves." Dilan poked his finger into the powder and then licked it clean. He folded the paper up carefully and returned it to his pocket. "We're going down in history, Brother. The founders of a new order where everybody is freed from the lie, and everyone can enjoy the enlightenment of the holy powder."

Ivan studied Dilan for a moment in the cold. The bloodshot eyes withdrawn into his skull from years of drug use. His brown hair unwashed for days poking out in spikes from under his black baseball cap. He could almost feel a sense of regret for teaming up with the radicals. Suddenly his blood rushed from his head being amplified by the speed. The crystal methane rocketed his pulse as the rush pushed his thoughts away. The surge of energy, plus the lack of sleep, removed all his conscience he had formed in his youth.

Dilan, noticing Ivan's eyes roll a little, spurred him on, "Yeah man, feel it hit you. Feel the power! No one can stop us man, NO ONE! We're invincible."

"Yes, yes we are. It's time for 'one for one.' Let's go even the score." The two men walked out on to the sidewalk calmly and down the block in perfect stride with each other like soldiers marching. The wind blew strong with its freezing chill as the two held up at the second-to-last door before the corner of the block. A Ford Econoline van was outside with all the doors locked and the motor running. It was outfitted with some thermal heaters to keep the food inside warm for the catering company it was in front of.

The sign for the business was not illuminated but the lights in the room behind the rather small reception area were on bright. Ivan tried the front door. It was open as he suspected. The two men walked in. The warmth of the front area hit the outside of their skin and started to remove the chill from them as they rubbed their hands for friction. A Latin man struggled out the door from the food preparation area in the back room with a heavy stainless steel container. He looked at Ivan and Dilan but kept walking by pushing his back into the front door to open since his hands were full, and went to the van, setting down the container and fumbling for some keys.

Ivan walked guardedly behind the counter and into the back room. The area was a complete kitchen with all heavy-duty appliances like in a restaurant. One Latin man was carefully cutting a cooked turkey breast and arranging it on a silver platter. The other occupant of the space, a bone-thin Asian girl, toiled at the sink washing huge dishes unaware of the uninvited company. The Latin man paused momentarily, looking up.

"Hello," Ivan said, "Where's the boss?"

The man shrugged his shoulders, "No Inglés Señor." He pointed to a door at the rear of the cooking area. Ivan nodded and smiled an unspoken thank you. He walked up to it with Dilan shadowing him, and tried the handle. The door opened and he walked into the office. A startled man at the desk looked at the two men entering his office and cupped his hand over the receiver of the phone he was talking on, "We're closed!" he said authoritatively. He stared at them glaringly, not saying anything more.

Dilan pulled the door to the room shut. Ivan mischievously smiling reached forward to the phone's cradle and disconnected it.

"You got fucking balls, Punk! I said we're closed, now I mean it, get the fuck out of here!"

Dilan strolled around the walls of the room looking at the pictures. Several hung on each wall. Some promotional ones with salesmen shaking hands with the boss. He stopped at one in particular, one with a picture of the mayor of San Francisco and the boss of the catering business shaking hands. Dilan read the caption on the bottom, his voice hyped up from the adrenaline and speed. "Congratulations, big brother, you did it." Dilan laughed. He reached up and grabbed the picture off the wall and waved it around.

"Quit that, put that back!" Larry Bennard's little brother Kevin lunged out from behind his desk and wrenched the picture out of Dilan's hand and then pushed him, gesturing at the door. "You're on private property, now get out or I'll call the police."

"I don't think we're leaving just yet." Ivan thundered grabbing Kevin Bennard by the hair with one hand and the throat with the other, tossing him back against the wall into the corner.

Kevin jumped up and reached for the phone but Ivan shoved it off the desk causing it to crash to the floor.

"This is illegal, you can't do... you'll be in big trouble!"

"Convenient, don't you think Dilan, opening a catering business a week after your brother is elected mayor? Kinda guarantees good business. Nice fat contracts for all the city's functions. And there are so many city functions aren't there? How much of a kickback does big brother get? Kevin."

Kevin stood in the corner listening angrily.

"What about the other legitimate catering businesses? Doesn't it seem unfair to them? Do they get any of the taxpayers' money spent on their services?"

"Hey, you don't like it, vote for Ross," Kevin said arrogantly.

"We don't vote," Dilan said.

"How much you paying those people out there, you fucking piss-ant?" Ivan asked "Three fifty... Four dollars? They don't speak English so it can't be much."

"It's none of your business."

"Well we're making it our business. We don't feel it's fair, in fact we feel we need to do something about it."

"Who are you guys?" Kevin asked challenging, "You have no idea what you're messing with!"

Ivan, having enough of the conversation, planted his feet wide and swung a roundhouse at Kevin, grazing his forehead causing his head to bang against the wall. Kevin darted forward trying to split between Ivan and Dilan, but Dilan grabbed one of his legs at the thigh and hugged onto it causing Kevin to stumble to the ground. Ivan jumped on his back grabbing around his neck in a strangle hold. Kevin flailed his arms wildly on the floor with the two men on top of him. He struggled desperately, pulling with both arms on Ivan's chokehold but couldn't budge it while his face turned red from lack of oxygen. Dilan gathered up the other leg and held him from getting to his knees. Slowly a minute, then two goes by. Ivan finally let go. Kevin's dead body lay motionless on the floor.

Dilan got to his feet, "What about the other three?"

"Let them go. They've done nothing wrong. We have no war with them."

******

Steve pulled down the dark alley to his loft's garage. He clicked the button on the visor and the garage door slowly rolled back automatically energizing the lights inside. The rain subsided like a blanket being pulled back as he parked the Audi under the protection of the shelter. He turned off the ignition and reached for the handle to the door when his eyes glimpsed movement in the rearview mirror. Quickly he hit the garage door remote causing it to come down. Trying to look casual he looked in all three of his mirrors, but couldn't see anyone. "OK, big Steve, one movement." Reaching across his torso with his right hand he opened the door while simultaneously pulling his Beretta 9mm from the small of his back with his left hand. The door opened slowly at first, and as soon as Steve got one foot on the ground he exploded charging the rear of the car in the garage. Two big bounds and he thrust the gun down over the trunk hitting the figure that he hoped wasn't there but was, hitting with the barrel in the shoulder knocking it over to her back. Steve's eyes strained to focus before he shot the hit-man. . . .

Lifting the pistol away, taking a second to get control of his breath, Steve rubbed his eyes with his free hand.

"I wanted to see you. I don't know what they told you, but I'm not a bad person."

"Why should I care? I'm not one of your peers." Steve answered.

"They let me go. No one's watching me

anymore."

Steve walked up the stairs replacing his pistol to his waist. Gena McGrath followed him up, her long pearl white raincoat squeaking as she went up the steps. The extremely beautiful woman was only slightly tarnished by a splotch of mud on her buttocks and back from where Steve had mistakenly knocked her over.

Steve entered his loft, throwing his coat on the floor, and punching the lights to turn them on, heading straight for the kitchen, not looking back at his guest at all. "You want a drink?" He inquired as he reached into the cupboard and produced a glass. He opened the freezer and removed a bottle of vodka. She didn't respond, only stopping at the entrance to watch him pour a drink.

"I'm in trouble, I think?"

Steve just looked at her, studying her carefully, no need in answering an obvious question. He sipped the vodka out of the glass, the burn of the alcohol warmed his throat all the way down.

"The mayor loves me. Look. Here's a picture of us together." She reached in her pocket and pulled out a photo.

Steve, unimpressed, "Go ask him, don't bother me."

"He wouldn't see me!"

"There's your answer."

"What did he tell you?" Gena asked very concerned, teary eyed.

Taking another long sip on the glass Steve just stared back.

"He wouldn't hurt me, would he?"

"Well," Steve stroked his beard, "I take it you had sex with him, from this love statement you claim. That makes you mistress to his supposedly happy marriage, in an election year no less. Your old love, or crush, whatever you want to call Ivan is an anarchist who wants to overthrow the government. Let's see what else? The shooting of Jack Swanson. You know all of the details that aren't supposed to get out. Add to that you're surrounded by blood-thirsty vipers making power plays for their political lives. Do I need to spell it out for you?"

Gena looked down at the floor, her voice soft and sorrowful, "I'm. . . ."

Steve's conscience, burned out of him a long time ago, was bothering him for the first time since he could remember. She wasn't an anarchist. Her intentions weren't to hurt a single person. She was just a lonely girl caught up in this mess. She thought she was in love and got burned. America's seventy percent divorce rate was her pardon for that crime.

"They're going to kill me aren't they?" Gena

choked out the words between the tears.

"Ah, Ahm...No...Don't listen to me. I don't know anything, Gena... Sorry... Ah... I don't get out much, my manners are bad." She stared at him, so sad, it was killing him. It was like he was a doctor who just told a shining radiant young girl she was terminally ill. "Me and my big mouth," Steve cursed himself under his breath. "Let me get you a drink Gena," he said to the sad, sad eyes reflected from the face of the broken girl wet with tears. He walked back to the sink fumbling with the vodka bottle again, "Yes, have a drink, Gena. It doesn't fix anything but it seems to help." After pouring the second glass, Steve looked up to an empty loft, the door drawing its last inch shut.

It bothered him to see her, a casualty of this bullshit fucking war. He dumped her drink into the sink. It reaffirmed his distaste for these people who thought they could play God. The untouchables. He stared across the large room, thinking, planning. Master Thief, a robber. Robber of money. Robber of power. Killer.

Steve walked over to his coat he dropped on the floor and removed the note pad he had taken from the Eden Hotel. He decided he was going to keep pursuing Ivan till he could think of something better. He took the pad in the kitchen and removed a glass box from below the sink and set it on the counter. Holding the pad up to the light he inspected it carefully, looking for impressions while sipping his drink. Seeing none, he set the pad in the glass box. Going back to his junk drawer he removed a large bottle of super-glue and squeezed the entire contents onto a paper-towel. He put the paper-towel in the glass box and shut the door making an airtight seal. Steve checked his stove clock and went over to his entertainment center to watch TV.

The rain kept coming relentlessly as it always did at the beginning of Winter. It pelted the large bay windows of his loft. Steve felt so comfortable in it he just wished these problems would go away, and he could enjoy a normal life.

He thought about Gena. A young beautiful girl probably bored with her life. She would be a treasure as a girlfriend to someone who could handle her. Her karma wasn't with the anarchists. How she got screwed up hanging around them, he couldn't imagine. We have all been lured into the wrong circles at one point in our lives. Sad for Gena though, this one was too far gone.

Steve sipped the vodka made thick by the freezer while he reflected. The TV late night talk show gabbed along. He just stared at the screen the words going right past him. A sprawling news caption ticker-taped across the bottom of the screen. ..."More news concerning the murder of mayor Bennard's brother Kevin Bennard at 12:30am Pacific Standard time...."

Steve's eyes opened wide in surprise as if he had seen a ghost. He read the caption again as it scrolled across. Mumbling to himself out loud, "Oh man, if the shit didn't hit the fan by now, it just went into the blades and sprayed across the room."

He quickly ran several scenarios through his head, then dismissed them all. They were probably looking for him, but they were probably looking for a lot of people. The next couple days were going to be a Chinese fire drill of political power plays and posturing. People were going to be squashed like ants. Steve killed the entire glass of Vodka and got up from his sofa restlessly. He was excited. The more confusion and mistrust, the more his chances of toppling the established organizations. This was just what he needed.

******

Nova Santiago walked slowly up the S shaped path lit by micro lights on the sides to the ocean beach estate. The mailbox said "The Morris's" on the side, but it meant nothing. Richard Morris's marriage had long since dissolved from his womanizing and drinking to all hours of the night. Shoeghit's prostitution connections had tipped him that the mayor's chief of staff called for companionship on Saturday nights when he finally finished his six day week. He had been saving that little piece of information, not too sure how he could use it, but he knew now. It was war. This election was going to come down to the last man standing and Mayor Bennard was pouring a pair of cement shoes for the Jewish crime boss to be fitted for. Win or lose. Terrence had intercepted the call to the escort service on one of his scanners and had followed it with a call to the service canceling the appointment. Nova would don the guise of the whore tonight in place of the real girl.

Nova rang the door bell. It chimed for a second and then the door buzzed, opening itself. She let herself in. The interior of the beautiful house was centered around an elegant staircase that was done with all wood railings and carvings on every post. At the top of the stairs Richard stood in a burgundy robe looking down. Crystal glass in his hand filled with some cola colored liquid. "Come in dear. Pull the door shut behind you."

Nova did so also removing her trench coat and hanging it on a thin wooden coat rack. She was wearing a black and white mini dress that covered just above her butt. When she reached to hang her coat her two creamy tan buns popped out exposing herself and the lack of underwear.

She wrestled the skin-tight dress back down embarrassingly hiding her perfect ass.

Richard smiled, "Honey, that's the best looking thing I've seen all day. What's your name?"

"I like to be called Nova."

"Nova, I like that. You know what a supernova is?"

Nova did but she didn't want to come across as too smart, after all she was supposed to be a whore, she reasoned. "No," she replied as she walked up the stairs gracefully, her beautiful bronze legs shining in the light. "I'll do my best to be your Super Nova."

"Richard smiled, "I bet you will, Nova." As she got to the top of the stairs Richard reached out and helped himself to feeling between her legs. His warm hands fondled her naked vagina still slightly chilled from the walk up.

Nova tried hard not to flinch or act displeased by the older man feeling her. Especially the instant she walked within range of the pervert's arms. His breath reeked of alcohol even from five feet away. Richard kissed her on the lips, pushing his tongue into her mouth while simultaneously Nova insidiously squeezed an eye dropper of Chlorine-hydrogen into the drink he was holding. She tossed the dropper over the rail and then eased out of the kiss. "I'm going to fuck you over all night."

Richard smiled, "Honey you need to work on your English, it's 'fuck you all night.'" He grabbed her by the hand gently and escorted her to the bedroom.

4

Steve went back into the kitchen to look at his fume chamber. Reaching for the dimmer switch to the kitchen lighting usually set about half way, he dimmed it to a third of the power. The fumes from the glue stuck to all the fingerprints and depressions in the notepad. Digging through in his junk drawer once more he pulled out a black light and shined it into the box. Like magic the words written on the slip that was torn-off appeared in faint impressions on the one below. "Blisters, Hot Little Number, Dee Dee, Last set one o'clock, Tuesday."

A strip-burlesque bar on Valencia St. An edgy place with a quick-on-the-draw crowd. Steve had seen a few of their shows since it opened a couple of years ago. Erotic Theater, the newest rage in the smut bars. Europe had had it for years, but we had just discovered it. It made going to the nudie bar a little more justifiable than when you just went to slobber around a stage and stick dollars in some tired broad's G-

String. That shit wouldn't fly at home with the wife or girlfriend.

Looking at the stove's clock: midnight. "I need to get down there now." Steve bolted from the kitchen seizing his coat from the floor and reseating his pistol in the small of his back as he barreled down the stairs to his garage. He mashed the door activator and crammed into the Audi. The garage door rolled back opening to the alley in the Lower Market area of the city. Steve revved the engine while turning the lights on. To his dismay he saw in his rear view mirror that a homeless man had set up camp against his garage door. He had rolled his shopping cart up to the door and strung a blanket from it to the garage, tying it off to the door handle. When the garage opened, it had pulled the blanket right up with it and spilled the shopping cart over.

"Fuck it all to hell," Steve screamed inside his Audi, the sound muffled from the outside.

The homeless man scrambled to his feet awkwardly in the layers of cloths he had on. "God Damn You, God Damn You!" he yelled as he stepped into the garage and banged on the trunk directly behind the car, blocking Steve's exit.

Steve rolled his window down, motioning the man to come to it. "Come here damn it!"

The homeless man kicked Steve's fender and walked angrily up to the driver's side of the car. "You owe me man, you owe me big! You're gonna have to pay for that. And I'm hurt, call me an ambulance right now!"

Steve kept waving his arm for him to come closer. "Come here. I'm hard of hearing. I'll get you an ambulance. What's your name friend?" Steve held his cell-phone up and waved it at him.

"Harvey, and I want your name you oppressive white fuck!" The man yelled with slobber spitting out of his mouth.

"My name's Wall Banger." The homeless man Harvey stopped raving for a second and looked at him oddly.

Steve thrust his arm at the homeless man grabbing the collar of his jacket in his left hand with an iron grip and throwing the Audi into reverse with his right. "Yeah. what's the matter?" Steve screamed at him as he drew him close to the window, "Haven't you ever heard of a Harvey Wall Banger?" Steve mashed the accelerator, causing the front wheels to spin, smoking and screeching.

The Audi raced backward crashing into the shopping-cart, launching it into the air ten feet to the other side of the alley, spewing its contents all over the ground. Steve held on to Harvey as he dragged alongside the car against the door, unable to keep his feet under him. He hit his shoulder violently on the side of the garage as the Audi cookied circularly into the alley. Steve pushed the remote to close the garage while he kept backing away from it dragging the homeless man alongside the car. "Come on!" he yelled at the man, "Don't you get it? Harvey Wall Banger. Ha! Fuck head!" He finally threw him away from the car after dragging him thirty feet. The man slammed to the ground like a baseball player sliding along a couple feet and then grabbed his knee.

Steve stopped and threw the car into drive and sped past him missing his legs by only inches. "There, now you're hurt. You can call an ambulance legitimately. And just think, you don't have to lie. You should thank me for that." The Audi fish-tailed out onto Third Street and darted off for the Mission and Valencia Street.

******

12:15AM Saturday. The pilot of the DC-10 came on the intercom, "Good evening.If you haven't noticed I've activated the fasten-your-seat-belts sign. We will be beginning our final approach into Oakland International Airport at this time. We're on time, so those of you making connections on different airlines shouldn't have any difficulties."

Touw looked at his watch trying to calculate

how long it would take to get to the storage locker he kept in Hayward. They said they were open twenty four hours, he thought. We're going to call them on that, tonight.

When Touw got word in Hawaii there was trouble, he didn't hesitate to come back. The innocent looking young Asian man loved a good fight. Looking at him you wouldn't think he could hurt a fly. He looked about as deadly as Don Knotts. He enjoyed using that to his advantage. Dressed nicely and with red highlights in his black Asian hair he looked the part of an art student. Steve had instilled the necessity of being cunning instead of violent to solve problems. Touw favored violence, but realized Steve was right about only using it in certain unavoidable situations. If he hadn't heeded Steve's warning a year ago he would probably be in prison somewhere now. Steve had given him challenges, uses for his hate and anger other than random explosions. Focused him away from the randomness of his criminal career.

Upon talking to Steve he immediately bought a ticket back, flying into Oakland instead of SF. He paid cash and didn't cancel his other return trip ticket so as not to arouse any suspicion. As soon as they touched down he was going straight to a cab and have it drive him to the storage lockers. He kept a war car ready there for just such a situation. To Touw life was in the fight. The time between elevated states of consciousness in combat was just dying a slow death. There was a purity in combat. Violence.

The war car was a factory supercharged Buick Park Avenue Ultra. The kind of car a golfer might consider sporty. The perfect car to move around the city and not get noticed. A sturdy four door sedan, fast as a rocket. Satellite map display, two mobile phone hookups, and a fax. Touw had removed the rear seat and welded in a box under it for keeping a MAC-10 submachine gun and a Glock 9mm. It was totally hidden from sight when the seat was repositioned on top, but accessible while driving. He had also bolted on a small metal box, hinged on one end to the underside rear of the car just in back of the fuel tank. It was filled with tire spikes, activated by a spring-loaded latch that could be popped open by pulling a wire that ran under the carpeting of the interior to the driver's seat. Below the dash there was a rear-light kill-switch that would turn off the tail lights without turning off the fronts. Not quite 007. But not bad.

The plane navigated its descent into Oakland. Touw removed the phone from the headrest in the seat in front of him. He dialed Steve's loft, it rang three times and the machine kicked in. He dialed Steve's cell phone. It rang and then answered.

"Hello," the sound of a car's engine revving and then dropping off in the background.

"It's me."

"Ah, good, are you in for the night?"

"No, I thought I might go out. Just haven't made my mind up where."

"Do you remember that club we went to for Carlo's bachelor party?"

"Yes."

"Do you remember the club we almost went to instead of that club?"

"Yes."

"I heard that place was happening tonight. At least 'til one o'clock."

"I might be able to get there right then."

"Try. If not, stay in contact. I feel we're going to get lucky tonight."

"Sounds good, bye." Touw hung up the phone abruptly. "There. Try and trace that call motherfuckers." He returned the phone to its spot and elevated his seat up for the final approach.

******

After ditching the Audi, Steve entered Blisters, paying the twenty dollar cover without any reservations. The club was packed to overflowing. The crowds of men mingled shoulder to shoulder standing in all the spaces. A long bar with old creepy chandelier hanging down over it handed out the drinks as fast as possible to the thirsty patrons. Three different female entertainers were elevated on their display pedestals, dancing seductively in the front room of the bar. Their oiled-up bodies were completely naked except for the smallest possible G-strings covering their vaginas. The smoke floated through the bar like the fog on the bay. If they intended on making the place look evil they did a good job, Steve mused. He turned his torso sideways and shuffle-stepped carefully through the crowd trying not to step on too many feet before he made it to the bar.

The bartender closest approached him, an Indian man proudly wearing his returban. "What do you want?" he yelled over the deafening noise of the music and crowd.

"Seven and Seven," Steve yelled back.

The bartender put the drink together with rapid-fire moves.

"Hey, have you seen Ivan tonight?" Steve yelled across the bar.

"I don't know an Ivan," the bartender replied, sliding the drink to Steve's hand and grabbing the money from his other hand.

"What about Hot Little Number, did she dance yet?"

The bartender, already asking the gentleman to Steve's right what he'll have, quickly responded.

"She's in the back room," and then ignored whether Steve responded to him or not.

Steve grabbed his drink, taking a sip before he started for the back room. "Damn, you think you could water it down a little more?" he protested. "Boy, I guess I won't have to worry about a DUI will I?" The bartender didn't acknowledge the comments.

"Why are you looking for Ivan?" a voice barely discernible over the noise, asked him.

Steve looked over his left shoulder at the skinny man asking him. The telltale signs of drug use flashed across his face like a neon sign. Sunken eyes, withdrawn cheeks. "I need to talk to him."

"Why?"

"Why? Because, that's why." Steve looked hard at-the enquirer. He despised junkies, especially ones that thought they were tough.

"Well you'll never find him. Never!"

"Yes I will. He's a part of the revolution. He'll come to me eventually. But I can't wait for his normal contact time. Some information has come up he must be advised of."

"Are you his contact?" the drugged out man asked.

"Why? Who are you?"

"I'm Dilan. Didn't he tell you about me? I'm part of his cell."

"Ah yes, Dilan, he did mention you," Steve smiled like an adult would smile at a kid. He offered a handshake.

"I finally get to meet my contact. The beard and the long hair—I should've known it was a disguise. Well what's happening? What do I need to know?"

Steve thought for a minute, "I can only tell Ivan. Sorry Dilan, I don't know you well enough yet. Where's Ivan?"

"I don't know. I'm supposed to meet him at the Eden Hotel on Wednesday."

"That's no help. What good are you as a soldier?" Steve roared, "How can we get anything done when you're all fucked up on drugs. Look at yourself, look at your bloodshot eyes. Now go away."

Dilan looked at him hatefully for the scolding, then walked off into the crowd. His leather jacket and ball cap blended into the mass of people.

Steve studied the crowd momentarily then maneuvered carefully through the tide of people to the back room, trying not to spill his drink. The sleazy socialites were at the height of inebriation in the wee hours of the Saturday morning.

He pushed his way through the heavy curtain drawn across the door into the back room. An elaborate gothic stage with grotesque gargoyle statues leaning over each side towered over a space for about three hundred people full to capacity. Spikes from the back of the stage topped with two foot long candles illuminated the background as seven naked women in knee-high boots strutted back and forth across the stage, inciting the crowd. Rows of drunken men four deep pushed against the stage with their money in their hands stretched out for the girls to remove from them.

Working his way to the side, Steve put his back against the wall and sipped on his drink. He squinted to see the figures of the women dancing on the stage through the smoke. A booming voice came over the PA.

"Come on, Gentlemen! You got five more minutes before these vixens leave the stage for the last time. Show them how much you love them!"

Steve chuckled, fucking idiots, you would get more bang for your buck if you would just pay for a hooker. Look at those dogs. He laughed again. How the fuck am I going to get to her? He looked the crowd over. If Ivan were in this bar, he wouldn't be in this mess. Dilan seemed sincere about him not being here.

Steve shot the rest of his drink down his throat and tossed the cup on the floor. Moving through the crowd as fast as he could without drawing attention to himself he made for the exit. As he grabbed the exit handle on the door a hand grabbed him and yanked him around. Quickly Steve tensed all his muscles and widened his stance for balance to lay a rock-your-world punch on whoever it was.

"Why are you running boss?"

Steve looked down at Touw latching onto him by the elbow. "Ah, good, you're here. It's a madhouse up front. The girl we need to see is going off stage now. This was her last set and then she's supposed to hook up with Ivan, after. You have the car?"

"Yes."

"OK, pull it into the alley behind the bar and back as far as you can without losing sight of the rear door. Go!"

Steve walked out smiling like he enjoyed himself then ducked into the connecting alley two buildings down. The alley brightened as he walked down it, as the motion sensitive lights were activated. He stayed close to the walls circling around a number of dumpsters, turning left at where it T'ed to go to the back of the club.

He looked over his shoulder as he passed and spotted Touw pulling in at the end of the block. A single light radiated over a heavy green steel door. A few indentations at foot level showed that it had been tried as an entrance before. A recycling bin and a dumpster were placed against the wall to the back side of the alley so Steve hid down between them and waited. Excitement surged through his blood, the alcohol only inciting Steve's aggressive side further.

An engine started at the end of the alley. Steve peeked curiously around the corner of the recycling bin. Touw was leaving, backing up into the street. That's unlike him. He'd never quit when things got hot before. Steve looked through the darkness, letting all his senses absorb every movement and noise. On the roof of the building three down, something was moving. He eased back into his hiding spot. Someone else had done their homework. Homeless people don't climb onto roofs. Cops? A hit squad? Whatever it was, it wasn't good. Steve was trying to think if it was possible to have tailed him. Or they might of bugged his car. That had to be it.

A police sharp-shooter, or an assassin, would have a starlight scope that turned night to day. Steve got as far back as he could against the wall to hide, looking straight across the alley at the back windows of a garment building for reflections. A couple of figures moved about behind the dirty panes of glass.

The heavy steel door cracked open, music

escaped like water leaking. The voice of a girl said goodnight to her friends. Two beautiful girls walked past the small slit between the rubbish cans Steve was backed into. They had their sweats on and were toting large gym bags on their shoulders. The figure of a huge bouncer followed behind them, escorting them to their car. The door squeaked as it drew shut, muffling the music again from inside, then opened again, the music surging back. Steve tucked as far back as he could, but was unable to see the two figures. Boom! The sound of the back door of the garment factory burst open, scuffing feet scrambling out into the alley.

"Freeze! Don't move." A pause of silence for a second, a second is an infinite time in deadly situations. Six people's minds were racing with panicked ideas of what they should do.

"Up against the wall both of you." Another second went by and then the faint sounds of a couple of footsteps to the wall.

Steve, looking out his small space, was suddenly and painfully hit in the nose with the barrel of a pistol. "You get out of there too." The figure, now visible, was pointing a gun to Steve's head between the trash bins. Steve stood up raising his hands. The man grabbed him by the collar and yanked him forward out into the alley and then up against the wall next to the girl and man. It was the mystery man all right, Ivan. Steve was so mad at himself for doing the dirty work for Shoeghit. Now it was hitting him he was going to do some time too. All three were spread-eagled against the brick wall to the back of the club. The shadowy figures of the men hovering behind them stayed out of their line of vision.

At the entrance to the alley a van entered, its lights bright at first but then the driver turned them off, leaving only his hazards on. It pulled up and stopped just shy of the back door to the club. No one said a word as the driver got out, walked to the other side and opened the cargo door. "You aren't cops," Steve challenged, trying to look over his shoulder. "Who the fuck are you?"

Bam! The butt of a gun pistol whipped the crown of Steve's forehead, knocking him to the ground. He cradled his head in pain.

"AH!... Fuck you guys, fuck you guys all to hell! Kill me here you sons of bitches. Steve, using his magician's gift of distraction, flailed his left arm angrily at them in defiance while drawing his pistol from the small of his back with his right.

"Don't move asshole! You only get one warning."

"Then give it to me motherfucker! Touw!

NOW!" Steve screamed, not knowing if Touw was around or not. BA,BA,BA,BA,BA... The sound of the full auto MAC-10 spraying bullets mowing down the three men standing over them like bowling pins. Bodies lifted off their feet and slamming hard to their backs, their limbs contorting in all kinds of unnatural directions.

POW! The sound of a cannon going off from the direction of the roof as Dee Dee's head exploded like a watermelon, blood and brain fragments everywhere. The headless body fell to the wall crumpling into a heap. Ivan dove to the rear door of the club in a somersault roll. It immediately opened and he tumbled in.

Steve capped off two shots at the figure on the roof while scurrying on all fours toward the front fender of the van. The man who drove it up and got out to open the cargo door dove into the back as soon as the shooting started. Leaning up against the front grill, Steve peeked quickly in the front window of the van. The man was trying to slide into the driver's seat keeping his body lower than the dash. Steve put his pistol point-blank against the front window at a downward angle aiming it precisely, Bam! Bam! The Beretta jerked in his hand back twice. The figure of the man disappeared below the view of the dash. Blood spots were visible on the seat. Steve looked the alley over fast. He was the last man standing.

"Touw! The roof! Cover me!"

No verbal response but a blast of full-auto machine gun fire from where ever Touw was hiding out. Steve took off running into the darkness as fast as he could. An all out sprint to the light at the corner three buildings down. Boom! The assassin's cannon went off. The bullet from the huge rifle crackled by his ear. He could feel the vortex from its velocity pull on his shoulder as it missed by inches, hitting the pavement in front of him causing sparks to spray into the air.

The legs of his solidly muscled body propelled him right around the corner, running so fast he couldn't turn sharp enough to stay on the sidewalk and went into the street. He stayed in full sprint rounding the next corner, heading back to the front of the club. A few people were milling around the entrance looking up in the air wondering where the popping noises were coming from. A taxi was double-parked picking up a fare, a young couple getting in the back.

Steve could see his Audi on the other side of the street only a hundred feet away as he ran by the curious on-lookers. He passed the cab running as hard as he could when he heard screaming over his shoulder. He looked back, his gun ready to fire, only twenty feet from his car.

Ivan had the cab driver in a head lock and had just pulled him out the window of his cab. Dilan had the back door of the car open and was removing the passengers at gun point.

Steve hopped and skipped trying to stop his momentum but it was pointless as he watched the two men disappear into the car after depositing its occupants rudely on the street. The cab took off up the street barreling recklessly through the intersection's blinking red lights.

Switching his Beretta to his left hand, Steve quickly dug his keys out of his pocket and rammed them into the door's slot setting off his car alarm. In one incredible display of coordination he jumped into the driver's seat, inserted the key and turned it, and slammed the Audi into drive. The motor literally started in gear, sputtering for a second at the strain, then the flood of fuel from the floored accelerator rocketed the cylinders, pegging the tachometer. The Audi jumped and bounded as the spinning front wheels turned hard to the left, griping the pavement, fish-tailing him around in the direction of the cab.

Steve could see the tail lights of the speeding cab bouncing exaggeratedly ahead as it sped over the uneven streets. His Audi was gaining speed at twice the pace of the Chevy. The speedometer climbed and climbed unnervingly. Big city streets and high speed didn't mix well. Holding his breath as the car blurred through the intersections he attempted to put on his seatbelt but then gave up.

The cab locked up its brakes and slid around a corner to the right, disappearing from sight only two blocks ahead of Steve. He swerved the car into the empty oncoming traffic lane to get a less sharp angle on the turn and take it at a faster pace to gain on them. The buildings blurred by as he coaxed the Audi around the corner, the tires chirping warning they couldn't hold on to the pavement much longer. He straightened it out only a half a block back from the taxi cab, mashing the accelerator for that extra bit of speed he needed.

Ivan, not even letting off the gas at the intersection, strained the cab to its max, blue smoke coming out of the tail pipe from the engine not being able to burn all the gas.

A Trans Am crossed the intersection seconds before the speed yellow bullet of the cab t-boned it on the passenger door smashing it through half the car and sending it diagonally out of the intersection onto the sidewalk. The cab's front hood and fender crushed all the way to the dash kept heading straight in the same direction bleeding off its momentum.

Steve looked on in horror, as his car traveling

over a hundred miles an hour transected the distance in a split second, smashing the rear of the cab, the hood of the Audi compacting straight up, air-bag catching his body as it left its seat like a missile heading through the window. Everything went black as the men could only hear the sounds of the tires screeching to a stop. The cars sprayed across the street like a bomb had gone off at the intersection. Glass and pieces of mangled metal everywhere.

Having no idea how long he sat dazed in the car, someone shook Steve and screamed at him.

"Get out, get out now!"

"Don't touch him, wait for the ambulances."

"Fuck you lady!"

"Aaaa.." the high pitched scream of a lady aggravated the nerves at his brain stem.

"Ah shit what happened?" Steve expounded looking into the deflated air bag.

"COME ON!" Touw screamed wrenching Steve's arm out the window with all his might. A lady was beating him on his head with her purse.

"Stop it, stop it, you're going to kill him!"

Touw pulled Steve through the window and onto the ground. He grabbed Steve's right arm putting it behind his neck and drug him to the war car sitting at the edge of the accident with the engine running. Steve, dazed, looked back as Touw opened the door to the Park Avenue and plopped him in. The well-meaning lady grabbed hold of both sides of his neck while Touw scrambled to the other side of the car quickly.

"Support the neck," She said, "You have to support the neck in case there's whiplash."

Over her shoulder the smoking wreck of the cab sat there up against a group of cars, empty. No Ivan, or Dilan. In irritation, Steve tried to look around the lady who was holding him by the neck. No sign of them, just an ever growing crowd. About ten people were surrounding the red Trans Am that got T-boned. Hit so hard it was almost sliced in half. No one was making any effort to help the driver or passenger, looks like they're dead, Steve thought, upset with himself.

Touw slammed the door shut hard rocking the car. He grabbed one of the lady's hands and pushed it away, "I'm taking him to the hospital!"

"How dare you?" she replied grabbing back a hold of his neck, "He's waiting right here 'til an ambulance with trained medical technicians can look at him."

A block back an SFPD black and white turned the corner then accelerated straight at the scene of the accident.

"My apologies in advance!" Steve expounded while he reached up and grabbed her by both wrists and pushed her back out the door, spinning his legs around into the car.

Touw floored it. The timid looking sedan jolted forward, the G-force shutting the passenger door automatically. The Buick darted away up the block to the right of the wreck. The muffled engine's factory supercharger engaged, letting its presence be known by a soft whistle and a wrenching burst of power. The buildings quickly began to blur by again, Touw's attention riveted to the road in front of him.

Steve, stiff but getting better by the moment, twisted his torso in the seat to look behind him. The accident scene was rapidly getting smaller and smaller, but the strobe lights on the top of the police car weren't. "They didn't buy our story that we were going to the hospital, they're pursuing us."

Abruptly Touw looked in the rearview mirror and then back at the road. He reached for the tail light kill switch under the dash, while letting off the accelerator, braking slightly and maneuvering a corner. Steve held on for all he had as the big car dove around and then straightened out. The engine red-lined again as they blasted down Army Street.

"Every cop car in the city is looking for us by now!" Steve barked. "We need to get out of this car!"

A cop car coming up Army street toward them

appeared. It stopped as they sped toward it in the other lane. "Any ideas?"

"Yes!" Touw fired back, too busy to explain.

They blasted by the cop car that immediately U-turned and began pursuit with the other cop car a block back. Army Street opened up into two lanes with no traffic all the way to the bay. Touw reached down pawing the floor board for the wire, grabbed it and pulled it. Steve looked back as hundreds of tire spikes sprayed across the road bouncing everywhere. The Buick exceeded a hundred and kept accelerating. Army Street dipped down as it went under the freeway, making the Park Avenue lift off its wheels airborne over ten feet then smash to the ground crunching the frame to the wheels. Touw manhandled the car back into control not letting off the gas at all.

"Are they still coming?!"

The red and blue strobe lights on top of the police cars grew smaller in the distance. "No, but that's only a temporary fix."

Touw let off the accelerator, the Buick started to slow. Then he applied the brake and it slowed more. Steve looked over at him nervously, "What are we doing?"

"Yellow cab's home base is right here." He turned the Park Avenue calmly into an unmarked road leading off Army Street. Steve looked back barely able to see the flashing lights in the distance. "Don't worry," Touw assured, "the tail lights are out on the back. They can't see us. My sister works the graveyard shift as a dispatcher for Yellow."

After driving between a series of buildings the road ended in a gate. A booth for a security guard was empty now at this late hour. Touw calmly pulled up to the small box mounted on a post, rolled down the window and reached out to press the button. "Ah, hello? This is TouwLý. I came to drop something off for my sister WendyLý."

"Just a minute please," the box squawked back.

The two men sat anxiously in the car. Thirty seconds seemed like an hour. The sound of a couple of sirens blasted by just behind them on Army Street.

"Ok, pull in and follow the yellow lines to visitors' parking." The chain link fence activated slowly rolling back. Agonizingly they waited as they watched the rearview mirror of slowly approaching flashing lights. Touw inched the Buick right up to the gate measuring it so the minute it would fit through he could go. Finally it cleared and he briskly drove in, navigating the yellow line recklessly for an eighth of a mile to the main building then parking the car on the back side behind a van.

Steve felt a small bit of relief come over him as the chain link gate pulled shut. Looking off to the left at the employee parking lot acres long, with thousands of cars. "Good call, Touw."

The two tried to compose themselves before getting out. Steve pulled down the visor and looked in the mirror on the back of it. The normal injuries caused by an airbag exploding are a burn on the face, like a strawberry you get when you skin your leg. He smiled at his image looking back at him in the visor. The beard he had grown so fond of had prevented the friction of the bag from damaging his skin. He winked at himself, then closed the visor and got out.

"How do you feel?" Touw quizzed him as he shut his door.

"I'm going to live. I don't have time to be hurt at the moment." The two walked to the heavy metal door in the office area. "It's funny how when someone's trying to kill you, the little aches and pains don't seem to be such a big deal."

"Yes, I agree, it puts things into perspective."

Touw led Steve down the corridor to the door to the dispatch office. The two men walked in as the three women looked them over from the consoles.

"What did you do?" Wendy scoldingly asked.

"Can I talk to you in private?" Touw

responded.

"No, I want Liz and Shatobway to hear what you have gotten yourself into this time." The two coworkers looked on smiling, breaking away to answer the phone occasionally but more concerned with hearing the dirt on Wendy's little brother.

Touw blushed a little as if on cue, "We went out drinking, and we're heading home."

Wendy looked on with her arms folded in a judgmental position.

"When a CHP car started following us. We...we'd been drinking, and they turned their lights on to pull us over, so we ran for it and escaped," Touw shrugged his shoulders as Steve looked on studying their expressions. "It made sense at the time," he insisted.

A moment of silence passed then the three women burst out in laughter. Steve smiled slightly as a kid would, having been caught raiding the cooky jar.

"And so you want me to bail you out? Or wait, even better, you want me to loan you my car. Ha!"

"I'll take them home," Shatobway said sympathetically. "I'll be off in an half an hour."

Wendy lectured Touw pointing a finger at him angrily, "Get it together! I'm tired of you screwing up! I'm off at seven, you better get your sobered up ass back here in a cab by then, or I'll have your car towed!"

Steve smiled at Touw. The two had once more dodged another bullet.

5

The drive home was tedious, with Shatobway driving relaxedly through the empty streets of the early Sunday morning hours. Touw had extended an offer to use his place as a base to work out of but Steve insisted on going home. "Don't be a fool," Touw said, but Steve would have none of it. He assured Touw that the Audi was registered to a guy who had died years ago and was untraceable. He removed his wallet from his pants and tossed the ID out the window. Then he dug out a new ID from the depths of his wallet.

Steve wouldn't admit it but he was upset with himself. One or maybe two people had been killed in the Trans Am. They had been innocently driving through the intersection going home. Civilian casualties in this intra-city war. The vipers in the battle *w*ho had willingly tossed their hat into the ring were of no concern to him, if they lived or died. But when innocent bystanders got killed because of the power plays of the greedy, that was unacceptable.

Shatobway's Honda pulled up to the bottom of Market Street a couple of blocks from the alley flat were Steve lived. "This is far enough, thank you Shatobway. Touw," Steve talked softly, "go home and get the car back. Keep your cell phone on and be ready to move."

Touw nodded, reaching up and squeezing Steve's shoulder as he got out. Steve politely shut the door and jogged across the Muni tracks toward his alley. He had a distinct feeling in his gut this might be the last night he would ever live to see. Might as well spend it at home for once.

Walking up onto the sidewalk Steve carefully navigated the junkies and packs of kids showing their tough guy badges as gang bangers. He kept his head down, acting unconcerned, blending in naturally to the atmosphere. Most of the lights of the businesses were out except for a few high-rises squeezing the last bit of life out of their employees at this hour. The liquor store Eldadsa, on the corner of Steve's alley had already locked up for the night. He peered in through the window. Savate was wiping up the counter and his wife was tallying the cash drawer. Steve gently tapped his key on the glass. The two looked up, startled, then saw that it was their friend and good customer. Savate put down his rag and walked to the door unlocking the bottom, cracking it open.

"We're closed my friend."

"I'm sorry Savate," Steve said, almost teary-eyed, "I really need a bottle."

Savate looked up and down the street briefly and then opened the door wide enough for Steve to slide through into the liquor store. "Come in. What's troubling you old friend?"

"Everything. The world. People. Life."

The two men walked to the counter, Savate's wife looked up from her accounting, "Oh, Hi Steve, a little late aren't we?"

Steve smiled faintly, finally relaxing in the company of friends. "Yes I'm sorry to put you on the spot."

"Not a problem for you old friend. What would you like?"

"This might be my last night in the City for awhile, so let's go with that bottle of Crown Royal, no wait a minute, get the Louis XIV off the shelf up there."

"¡Mi Dios!" Savate cried out, "You *are* in a drinking mood." He slid the ladder over and got the dusty bottle down. His wife rang up the tally, "One hundred twenty-two dollars, Steve."

He peeled the money off his cash roll and nodded in thanks as Savate escorted him to the door. "Drink some for me, old friend."

"I will, thank you."

Walking back out onto Market and round the corner into the darkened alley with his brown bag in hand, he watched the shadows around him cautiously. The cold night wind was blowing like a funnel down the alley as the rain had stopped for the time being. At the far end of the alley the lights of a Lincoln town car came on, followed by the engine starting. The car started down the alley rapidly and slowed only just before coming up to Steve. It stopped. The back door opened and a man in a suit got out. Steve squinted to see who it was, hoping he didn't have to break the bottle of Louis XIV over his head.

"Hello Steve," Roddy exclaimed through the darkness.

"What? What the fuck do you want?"

"Oh easy now. I don't want to become one of your victims." The wind blew Roddy's hair over his forehead, "You kill better than you thieve. You should be a hit-man, not a burglar."

"I need more time if that's what you're here for, now leave me alone, damn it!"

"The terms of the agreement have changed due to extenuating circumstances."

Steve glared at him through the wind, angrily. "Go on. I can't wait to hear this."

"We still want you to get Ivan, and kill him, but we want to clean up the entire mess since it's gone this far. This is spiraling out of control and nobody that has knowledge of the events can be left alive."

"And so?"

"We want you to kill Gena."

Steve didn't respond to the request.

"We expect this to be done by dawn. We can

make arrangements for the body to be disposed of."

"No, I'll handle it," Steve fired back. "You sorry fucks would leave it at the police station so you could have me framed...If I find her in the process of looking for Ivan I'll correct the problem."

"'*If* you find her' isn't going to be a problem. She's hiding under the fire escape to your apartment back there, waiting for you to get home. She's to die tonight. No loose ends. This is your huge mess you created. You fix it."

"You know Roddy, I'm happy I fucking made your lives a huge mess..."

"Be careful, little boy who thinks he's a man. Don't grow honorable on me. Did you hear the news? There's a cop killer on the loose. Three dead cops and two badly injured. I wonder if they would find anything linking you to the murder at your house, like DNA? Ah yes. Got your attention, didn't I?"

"Roddy...You errr..., you realize that you're a loose end too. I'm the one that is doing all the difficult work. You know everything but do nothing. It looks to me like all you are capable of is running your mouth. There's a whole world full of people that can run their mouth. Who would be easier to replace...? Ah yes. Got your attention now."

Roddy's squinty eyes glared furiously as he held back his rage. As if Steve had turned him off, he didn't add anything further to the conversation. He stared him down the entire time he was getting back into the back of the Lincoln. Steve didn't care. He had had about enough of this tough guy crap. The Lincoln drove off into the cold night.

The angry master thief walked the rest of the distance to his door, not looking at the fire escape. He grabbed his keys out of his pocket as the icy cold raindrops began to fall again. "Gena come in before you catch your death of cold."

A rustling under the fire escape produced the beautiful girl. She looked out of place in this stark environment.

Steve unlocked the door and held it open for her. She walked into the little entrance and up the stairs to the door to the loft. Steve was walking close behind admiring her legs, still shapely even with smudges of dirt and goose-bumps from the cold.

"Those pieces of shit think I'm going to kill this ray of sunshine," Steve thought to himself, "No, no way."

Entering the loft the warmth surrounded them as the thick door slammed itself shut. Steve rounded the counter into the kitchen turning the light up only enough to barely see. "Let's keep it a little dark in here. I don't want any prying eyes. Gena shivering slightly removed her expensive coat, now dirty, and lay it on the floor. Her large round breasts normally hidden under the office attire were only clothed in a silky button-up blouse. Her enlarged nipples were visible even from the kitchen, distracting him briefly while he poured a drink. She plopped down into his reclining chair, arms folded trying to retain some warmth. Steve sipped down a half a shot of cognac to warm up his insides.

"You shaking because you're cold or from nerves?"

"They ransacked my house," Gena responded somberly.

"It's a different kind of living having someone after you. How about a little drink to warm your bones?"

"I don't drink."

"You might want to start," Steve chuckled trying to take the edge off the situation.

"I want this all to go away. I can't take this anymore."

Steve didn't respond right away. It wasn't going to go away. And there wasn't any comforting news to tell her. The lights of a car driving down the alley panned shadows across the room. A slight reflection of tears running down the Gena's face caught Steve's eye.

"Fear and intimidation is part of this business," he took a draw on the cognac and hardened his voice, "You're going to need to get used to it."

"I don't want to be involved in this...this business."

Steve walked out into the main area of the loft solemnly. "I'm supposed to kill you."

Gena didn't respond, didn't even look at him.

"I won't. But someone will. You can leave if you like." Steve was tired of this depressing conversation. He had problems of his own to deal with besides hers. He walked off to the bathroom, unconcerned with her, turning his back. Talking to himself he tried to cheer himself up. She had wanted a revolution, well she got it. Not my fault. He pulled his shirt off revealing his solidly muscled body. The beretta was now plainly visible in the small of his back. Running steaming hot water in the sink he splashed it onto his face trying to revive his senses.

Wiping himself down he walked into the kitchen and got a refill on the cognac. Gena slowly got up and walked over to him like a ghost. The blank stare and floating gait froze Steve in his tracks.

"What if I go to the east coast, disappear," she enquired at arm's length. "Will they follow me? Hunt me down? Arrest me?"

Steve walked past her out of the kitchen and

into the living area. He softly mumbled "Yes," as if he did want to say it. "They'll always be coming after you. It's a done deal."

"How long do I have?"

"I don't know, fate is a funny thing. It never goes along with the plan. A day, a month, I don't know."

"You're a gangster. You can protect me."

"No, and no." Steve sat on the sofa and then turned sideways laying down on it.

"I want to help you. Let me go with you. They can't get me if I'm with you. We'll be a team. I'll make you happy. I'll watch your back...I'll let you have me, you know, let you fuck me whenever you want." Gena undid the top two buttons on her blouse revealing the top half of her large breasts. "Feel them. They're perfect." She leaned over Steve, laying on the couch, the two huge tits hanging out, nipples erect. "Steve, touch them."

A soft snore purred out of Steve's mouth as Gena discovered he had slept through the whole seduction.

Gena, amazed but not upset walked over and sat on the floor in front of the stereo turning on some soft music, as the rain pattered against the window in the late hours of the night. Steve adjusted and scratched as the music softly filled the room.

Still aroused, Gena removed her blouse completely so she was topless, still sitting. Danger always turned her on. She never realized it until now. Pulling her wrinkled skirt up to expose the tight underwear she had on tonight she rubbed and fondled the outside of the clitoris through the underwear, making her wet.

Looking over at Steve still asleep, she dug her finger under her tight panties and fingered herself just feet from where he lay on the couch. The chance of getting caught aroused her more and more. Gena stood up quietly and slowly pulled her underwear down to her knees so if Steve awakened she wouldn't be able to get them up in time to keep from getting caught. She hiked her skirt up and continued fingering herself on complete display in the middle of the living room.

Her arousal deepened. The large round breasts swollen like ripe melons, nipples extended out at an upward manner. She giggled slightly as she poked herself with her finger.

The exhausted thief gasped for every breath of rest on the couch unaware of the spectacle of foreplay taking place in the middle of his livingroom just feet from him.

Gena's first orgasm found her. The juices dripped from inside her. The warmth of the cum dripping down the inside of her legs while she stood on total display in the middle of the room made her even more aroused. Recklessly she pulled off her panties not caring if she woke Steve, deep down hoping he would jostle up and see her in the embarrassing predicament then take advantage of her.

Her passion overwhelmed her common sense as she walked to the head of the couch putting one leg up over Steve on the arm rest, exposing her pussy to full view as she pulled it apart wide in defiance of all the moral values her Mormon parents had preached to her. Her erotic sense of danger heightened as with only a couple of strokes of her vagina she had another orgasm. As her blood boiled and her pulse raced she fantasized about forbidden things like Steve waking up and throwing her to the ground. Holding her down with his overpowering strength and taking her. It was too much as she had her third orgasm.

Suddenly her arousal grew cold, and she realized what she had been doing. Ever so painstakingly she carefully removed her leg from straddling over Steve asleep on the couch and went about the room gathering her stuff. She looked back at him blushing with embarrassment ashamed of her nymphomania, then dashed into the bathroom. If Steve had only known about the performance he had missed, she pondered. If he had caught me, I would have let him do anything he wanted to me. Anything. Again she started to feel aroused at the notion, so she blocked the thoughts and cleaned the cum off the inside of her thigh.

After an hour of intense rest, Steve rustled to the soft music coming from the stereo. Peaceful and relaxing. He tried not to think of the predicament he was in. If only we could start time now and erase the last week. Rolling to his side on the couch he gazed over to the beautiful Gena looking though his CDs. The artsy loft of his, charged by the presence of a woman. Romantic music playing. It was like a dream. He even thought he could feel a sexual energy in the room but he knew better. It had been awhile since he'd gotten any. He wasn't hurting for women, he had just been too busy with the last heist. Don't read into things he cautioned himself.

Gena removed a CD, placing it in the system, turned off the radio so that the pleasant sounds of a soft piano entered the space. Steve just lay with his head down on his arm and stared at her.

"I'm sorry. Did I wake you?"

"No, that's all right. I don't mind."

Gena raised the volume slightly, the vividly colored displays bounced and dashed to the rhythm of the music.

Rolling up from his back to hunch over the side of the couch, Steve tried to realign his sharpened senses, pretending like nothing happened even though he had to admit to himself he was a little more drunk than he cared to be. It had no bearing on his performance. There's no sobriety test in the underworld. It was just a little embarrassing. One of his favorite musical pieces played back to him.

"*A Celtic Lament*...I figured you for Rock and Roll or New Wave. Do you have a bit of culture or was it a lucky guess?"

She adjusted the bass up a level, "I used to dance in Riverdance when I was young. I like all kinds of music, but this seemed to fit my mood tonight."

"And what is your mood?"

"Sadness."

Steve started to respond but stopped himself. He wasn't going to be bated into a cheer-up talk. He didn't have the energy and he was in as much shit as she was. Looking over at her, he just enjoyed the company for a fleeting moment. He realized it might be the last moment alone with a beautiful girl he'd ever have. The soft music infiltrated his body. Like a drug it took the edge off him. Getting up off the couch awkwardly, avoiding the table, he walked over and sat down beside her on the floor facing the stereo.

"Drop the treble some and listen for the string instruments to come alive out of the surround-sound."

Gena paused for a minute as if Steve weren't there. He didn't respond to her plea for relief from her anguish.

Steve wasn't at ease either. He felt an urge to comfort her, but knew it would all be lies. He hated liars and phonies, but that was what she wanted. Some insurance that everything was going to be OK, even though it wasn't.

Gena got to her feet aggressively walking to get her coat, almost stomping her feet like an upset grade school kid and started to leave. She looked at Steve, hateful as though he had betrayed her.

That's it, he thought to himself. I'll play ball. I don't want to lose this girl. He jumped to his feet and ran for the door, Gena bolted at the same time letting out an angry emotional scream. Steve cut her off to the door at the last second, throwing her hand back away from the handle.

"Stop it! Let me go!" she screamed, tears running from her eyes.

Steve grabbed hold of her in a protecting bear hug and held her from doing anything.

"Stop it! God damn you, let me go!" Gena burst into hysterical crying falling limp in his arms. She rested her head on his shoulder, the warm tears of sadness trickled off the beautiful girl's face onto Steve's skin. The sensation really drove home how lonely he had been all these years on the run. He picked her up off her feet and carried her up the spiral stairs to the balcony of the loft and tossed her on the bed.

Steve leaned over her, one knee on the bed looking down at the young girl in so much trouble. She lay there staring back at him. Her tears had stopped but the expression of hopelessness hadn't left her. She reached out and cupped her hand around the back of Steve's leg. She was saying "I'm your's," in not so many words. It was a funny world, Steve pondered. At what was probably the last days of his life he was given this beautiful girl.

He kicked off his shoes and lay down on the bed beside her. With Steve caressing her, his hands running through her long black hair, Gena moved over right against him, body to body. Even with their clothes on Steve could feel her perfect round breasts getting harder against his hairy chest. Her huge nipples poked into him like knives of nirvana.

With his arms around her he reached down to her butt squeezing it, to see how she would respond.

Gena moaned putting her head down onto Steve's chest.

He held still for a moment, hoping he hadn't gone too far or misread her intentions. He felt his groin being probed for its contents, bringing a seductive smile to his face.

Gena found what she was looking for and grabbed around it through his pants a number of times as if she was in disbelief of its size. She grabbed it repeatedly measuring the length by feel. Her mood changed noticeably.

Steve—never one for taking a passive stance—was already pulling her skirt up exposing the big round white buns. This girl was truly built. Rolling up on to his knees on the bed he peeled his clothes off while his audience, Gena, sat there and watched in amazement at the ripples of solid muscle slowly being exposed.

"I had no idea you were so solid."

Steve didn't respond verbally, instead he responded by demonstrating his strength by grabbing the dirt blouse Gena had on and tearing it off her slowly. The fabric ripped down the front of her, pulled taunt baring her breasts to view. Steve took the waist of her skirt and did the same. Gena sat passively, acting as if she could do nothing to stop him.

Throwing the tattered clothes to the floor, he paused for a moment to look at the exposed parts. The naked girl lay there still on his bed not hiding any of her body. Her eyes were swollen with torrid lust. Her large breasts pointed up screaming to be squeezed and fondled. A wet snatche's aroma of hormones told him to proceed. He leaned down touching her small triangle of bush hiding her pussy, pulling it apart, Gena moaned with pleasure.

"I'm your slave," she softly asserted. "Do anything you want to me."

******

Sunday morning, 7:30AM. SLAP! "Wake up you fucking slob."

Richard Morris, the Mayor's Chief of Staff foggily came to his senses. Feeling himself all stretched out across the bed he tried to pull his arms in and sit up, but couldn't. Blinking rapidly feeling nauseous and hungover, he looked around rapidly discovering he is bound to the bed.

"What the fuck?! Are you crazy? I'm not into this. Release me now!"

Nova was sitting at the small desk in the corner of the bedroom eating the breakfast she had cooked while impatiently waiting for him to come around. She had put it on a sterling silver tray and china setting usually reserved for visiting upity guests. She looked at Richard, grabbing a sausage and sticking it in her mouth like she was going to give it a blow job, then biting it off viciously.

"I did not request this. Now release me, you,

you dumb whore! Do you know who I am?"

Nova just sat continuing eating as if nothing had been said.

"What the hell's wrong with you, aren't you listening? Let me go now...!"

She glared back as if insulted by the question. Then she reached over to a Polaroid camera she had set out on the floor. Nova took aim and recorded Richard in his compromising position with a picture. Then she put the camera down and returned to eating.

"I'll have your massage parlor shut down, damn it! Don't you understand?" Richard was so enraged he regurgitated a little vomit from the anger. He looked at her for a moment, wondering what she was up to. "That's right. Just stare at me and eat my food. Is this your power trip? Fuck you, little bitch...OK...I respect your hustling abilities. I'll pay you off if that's what you want. I can set you up with an apartment and a monthly installment if you just let me go. Yes, this is embarrassing. You win, OK? You win!"

Nova looked at Richard all spread out on the bed helpless, slightly amazed at his unstoppable and unwise ego. She sipped her coffee carefully because it was still scalding hot and studied him. He was right, she was enjoying the power trip. Getting up and pacing back and forth around the bed with her coffee she looked down at her catch.

The big fish, she mused.

"Well, are you going to stare down at me all day or what?"

Nova took her coffee cup, held it out over his groin.

"Don't you even dare. I'll have you locked up for assault."

Slowly she tilted the cup so that the coffee was right at the rim ready to spill over.

Richard squirmed back and forth under the cup. "It's not funny!"

"Really?" Nova said her first words, "I think it is." Slowly she began spilling the steaming coffee onto his genitals.

"AH, SHIT, AH!!"

The entire cup poured out on to him, causing him to scream in agony.

"Ah! Fuck." Richard bounced up and down on the bed at the limits of his restraints.

Nova giggled like a young girl amused at something.

"God damn you, you fucking bitch."

The smile left Nova's face as she took the heal of her hand and mashed it into his abdomen, knocking the wind out of him. Richard gasped to regain his wind. He looked at her standing over him with her arms folded. There would be no more disrespectful outbursts from the mayor's chief of staff. Reality was upon him. He was in big trouble.

The wily hunter Nova strolled back and forth in front of her quarry. What a prize he was, the big wheel in the city stuck in her spider's web. That's the way she saw it. Helpless to whatever she willed. The electricity of the moment incited her blood.

"What's your name?" Richard asked politely.

Nova waited a second before she replied as if to reiterate she is in charge and didn't have to respond. "My name was Nova."

"That's a differen—"

"Why is it," she interrupted him mid-sentence, "You scum bag politicians can be threatening to kill someone one minute, and sound charming the next?"

"It's part of the job," Richard conceded. "The only way to get to the top."

"At last, the real Richard Morris shows himself. And how do you feel about this?"

"It's not right, it shouldn't have to be that way."

"Then why did you act like a sniveling asshole to me last night?"

He started to answer, but she cut him off.

"Why is because you like to be that way. You get off on fucking with people. Power. You slip yourself into the role and let it take control."

He didn't answer.

"How long have you been in politics?"

"Twenty five years."

"I bet you know all kinds of dirty secrets." Burrrt! The door buzzer sounded. Nova walked out of the upstairs bedroom to the crest of the stairs and pushed the entrance release. The sound of the front door opening terrified her captive. Someone was coming in. She's not alone, he thought. He lay helplessly on his own bed. Nova walked back into the bedroom.

"Who did you let in?" Richard asked, fear in his voice. "Don't let someone see me like this."

"Why," Nova asked smiling at his predicament, "Are you embarrassed? Trust me, the last thing you need to worry about is being embarrassed. Richard focused on the door not looking at her. A expression of horror spread over his face like a monster was going to appear.

"Hi Terrence!" Nova announced as he stepped through the door.

"Good morning Nova! Gee, what do you have here?"

"I would like you to meet the Mayor's Chief of Staff, Richard Morris."

"Boy, what an honor! Don't get up on my behalf."

"Be careful Terrence," Nova warned.

"Why is that?"

"He's in a bad mood. He threatened to kill me

earlier."

Terrence paused a moment looking down at him from the foot of the bed. "Not a man to mince words, I suppose." He reached over to Nova grabbing her by the back of the neck and pulling her head forward till their lips met. The two French kissed intensely for a minute, in defiance of courtesy to their captive.

Finally they broke apart, gasping for a breath. "So did Shoeghit say what to do with our little Richard?" Nova smiled looking down to see the expression on his face for letting the secret out. Richard's stare was transfixed on her, but he said nothing.

Terrence walked out of the room motioning Nova to follow him. Outside the room he shut the door and began to talk, he looked distressed. "This is more than I want to get involved with."

"What do you mean? We've already done what he asked. Let's take the cash and get out of here. Shoeghit's men can come down and retrieve their package."

"No," Terrence said assertively, "It's not like that with these guys. Not like when we worked with Steve and you did your job, then went home and forgot about it. These guys don't stop."

"I don't understand?"

"Now he wants us to use him to get to the mayor. Get in close to the mayor and kill him."

Nova's eyes opened wide in disbelief. "No way! That wasn't the deal. That's too much trouble."

"We have to do it or they will kill us."

"Give him the money back. I'm not doing it."

"He won't take it back, we're in, no alternatives."

"We'll be caught you know. We'll be the patsies." Nova began to cry then forced it back. "I wish I would have never left Steve. What was I thinking? Maybe he would help us. I'll try to contact him. Shoeghit can't be serious about killing the Mayor."

"Yes he is. The police are tailing Shoeghit continually now. He's on the hook unless something big takes him off it. If the mayor dies while he's under surveillance, it's a big step towards clearing himself and shifting the investigation. Or at least that's the way he sees it. And that leaves Frank Ross to walk right into the Mayor's office and appoint a new police chief and the whole thing goes away, right?"

"They'll lock us away for life in Folsom, while they eat at five star restaurants and drive around in their Lincolns."

Terrence nodded, "Yes, they will."

"We have to find a way out."

"There is no way out. Two of Shoeghit's Israeli hit-men are downstairs right now,"

Terrence pointed over the rail down to the hallway to the entrance. Two square-jawed men with short tight haircuts and thousand dollar suits stared back. He whispered to Nova, "They have pistols with silencers under their coats."

She turned her head away and walked back into the room abruptly. Terrence followed slowly back into the bedroom shutting the door behind him.

"Well Richard," Nova said, "apparently we've both got a problem."

He looked up from the bed inquiringly.

"Do you like Jews?"

"I don't understand," Richard said.

"Do you like Jews? It's a simple question."

"If your talking about Shoeghit, the answer is no. But he's more a devil or atheist than a Jew."

"Well, let us tell you a story about some thieves, Shoeghit, anarchists and your boss Mayor Bennard."

Terrence gazed over at Nova supportingly, "Yes, do it. Tell him everything."

"Now you see the problem, we're supposed to kill the mayor. But it's not by our choice, it's survival."

"Yes that's a huge predicament you got yourselves into." Richard acknowledged, "Where do I fit into this problem? I'm not going to help you kill the mayor. Forget about that."

"No," Nova said, "Help us get out of this mess. Set up Shoeghit in a sting, arrest him and get the DA to cut us a deal for a plea-bargain. Put us in protective custody 'til you arrest his entire crew, and we'll testify against him. Larry Bennard will win the election handily and you'll stake out your ground as a force in SF politics. You'll be a hero. You could even run for the office next term. Imagine the press. Nation-wide coverage."

Richard's attention was focused. Great men knew how to see the opportunity when it arrives.

"So will you help us?"

A long second went by, "Yes."

"Great, we're so happy!" Nova jumped up, the two thieves hugged each other as if they had won a prize. They felt as though they had exonerated themselves from their predicament. If politics were only so black and white. What they didn't see was the blood-thirsty stare from their captive. No smile or exhilaration crossed his face. Behind his eyes the demons of power were at play.

6

A black Lincoln town car pulled away from the estate of Richard Morris with five people tucked soundly into it. Through the empty streets of the early Sunday morning in San Francisco they traveled smoothly, uninterrupted by traffic. The City looked menacing as they approached it. The buildings lurked high above looking down on them knowingly. A black day in the history of The City was in the making.

"Will the Mayor be in his office today?" Nova calmly asked as she continued looking out the window of the car as it drove.

"Yes," Richard replied to her in the back seat, "Normally he wouldn't be in today but with the election so close and the death of his brother being investigated, he won't be at home." Richard pulled out a smart phone and tapped at its small keys. An itinerary displayed on the small screen. "He'll be coming out of a meeting and beginning his fund-raising calls shortly."

"City Hall should be empty today?" Terrence asked.

"Yes, only a couple of guards at the doors. Maybe a few janitors."

The Israeli gangster in the passenger seat turned and looked at the three captives in the back seat knowingly suspicious of their casual attitude. "There is a private entrance that goes directly to the mayor's office. You will use that. I will be accompanying you up the stairs and checking to see that the job is done correctly." He handed back a pistol with a silencer, no clip of bullets in it. "The silencer is quiet, but I'll be able to hear it." He held up the clip, "You have three bullets, put them all in the head of Mr. Bennard." He held up an Uzi in his other hand, "I have a full clip, if you don't finish the job correctly, I will. And let me tell you thieves, you don't want that to happen. You'll get your bullets when you walk in."

"What about me?" Richard asked guardedly. "I've done what you've asked."

The hardened Israeli looked at him peering back from the front seat, "What about you?"

"You're going to kill me too, aren't you?"

"Yes," the Israeli said without a hint of guilt in his voice.

"Why the fuck should I help you then?"

"You don't have to. The only reason you're coming is we need your thumb print for the door. Your thumb. Not you. Your choice, we can turn around and go back to your house. I'll personally remove your thumb along with several other body parts before killing you...."

"No, no, that's OK, I'll cooperate. I wish they

would have expedited the installation of the voice recognition locks."

"That's the first thing on Mayor Ross's itinerary," the driver asserted comically. No one laughed.

"Be thankful I'm practiced in the art of killing," the Israeli gangster interjected. "It will be a better way to die than rotting of old age. Die like a man, with the respect and dignity of battle."

The Lincoln circled City Hall deliberately. Normally crammed parking spaces were empty, with the exception of the ones in the front by the main doors. Only a smattering of cars were there, not more than ten. The Lincoln pulled to the back of City Hall and stopped in front of the rear entrance. The gangster with the Uzi stuffed it into his coat and got out of the car slamming the door. Nova opened the door and got out followed by Richard and Terrence in tandem. The Israeli motioned them in front of him. As they passed, he handed Terrence the clip of three bullets. Terrence immediately seated it in the gun and concealed it in his coat.

They nervously proceeded through the back door. It opened to a small room with a heavy metal security door. Richard removed his keys and inserted it into the slot. Turning the lock he pressed his thumb onto a square finger print identification pad. The box paused then beeped. The door latch clicked and Richard grabbed hold of the handle and pulled it inward.

A set of metal grading stairs led up to the second floor. Richard led the way trying to stay as far away from the Israeli as possible. On the second floor the small hallway was closed off except for two doors leading out of it. One was a nice oak door and the other a normal looking wooden door.

Richard tried the oak door handle, but it was locked. He reached into his pocket and got the key, opening it. He looked through as he cracked it open, "Hey Larry, how's the fund-raising going?"

Terrence moved in front of Nova pulling his gun out to his side. The Israeli exposed his Uzi and held it up aiming it at all three of them from behind, concealed midway on the stairs.

Richard walked in, Terrence stepped through behind him, but Richard turned around and pushed him forcefully back out the door slamming it shut. Terrence tried for the knob. It was locked automatically.

Through the door Richard's screams reverberated in the reception area, HELP! HELP! MAN WITH A GUN, HELP!

Terrence, momentarily stunned, looked back at Nova then took his gun and blasted the door handle with all three bullets. Splinters of wood flew everywhere and he gave it a shoulder, smashing it open. It swung free exposing the back side of the reception area to the Mayor's office. Richard had crossed the room and was exiting the front door. Terrence instinctively aimed the gun at him for a split second but realized it was empty when he pulled the trigger. Nova pushed by him crossing the large room in full sprint after the chief of staff.

"I need something to shoot with damn it!" Terrence yelled back at his captor. The Israeli lowered his Uzi reaching into his coat with his free hand and producing another clip. He tossed it to Terrence and then took up position in front of the exit with his Uzi at his shoulder. The door cracked open from behind the secretary's desk to Terrence's left. Two men in suits burst through it, guns drawn. They ran into the room carelessly as in disbelief of what they were hearing.

Terrence didn't have the clip seated fully in the gun as the cops yelled at him, leveling their guns, "Freeze!" not seeing the other man at the back door. Blaaat, Blaaat, the roar of the unmuffled Uzi exploded rocking the quiet room. The streams of bullets penetrated the officers' bodies violently entering the front of their torsos and splattering out the back, sending chunks of flesh and bones everywhere. Shards of cloth whirled through the air as their bodies fell slamming to the floor... dead.

Terrence looked at his captor ejecting the Uzi's empty clip to the floor and grabbing another from his coat.

"Oh no you don't!" Pop, pop, pop, Terrence fired the small silenced pistol at close range hitting the Israeli gangster in the head with all three shots. Terrence knew he had hit him all three times, but his body balanced momentarily before it fell to the ground, terrifying him for a second that he had missed even though he knew he couldn't have.

In awe Terrence looked around the reception area of the Mayor's office. There was no fixing it now. A blood bath and he was first chair in orchestrating it. His finger prints and DNA were all over the room. Disengaging the clip from the small pistol he looked down counting the rounds. The second clip the Israeli threw him was full. He had five rounds left. Ramming it back into the seat in the handle he ran to the window. The Lincoln was gone. The driver had heard the fire-fight break out and had hauled ass.

"Well I'm not hanging around either," he mumbled to himself as he paused for a minute to look the scene over once more. "They'll send me to the gas chamber for this," he contemplated. Bolting back across the room to the first dead cop he dug his hand into his front pocket to remove the keys. There were two rings of keys. One with a bunch of Industrial looking ones, and the other with an alarm tab and a large key that said Mazda on it. He took both of them and proceeded for the exit, when he heard a shuffling in the next room. Terrence ducked for cover behind a desk. Quietly he stayed even though every survival instinct told him to run.

The noise of the phone receiver being picked up was discernible. Breathing hard, his pulse racing Terrence strained to hear into the next room. "Mayor's office. Officers down send help... This *IS* ...the Mayor God Damn it!"

Mayor Bennard was in the next room. He would make an expensive hostage Terrence figured. Thinking it over for a second, hostage situations never worked out.

It bothered Terrence that the bastard politico was going to get out of this scot-free, though. All these people dying around him would just catapult him to more fame and riches. The carnage would make him look like a survivor when in actuality the Mayor did nothing. The cops will probably catch Terrence someday soon and make a spectacle out of him. The Mayor will use it and use it, over and over, for political gain.

Sorry motherfucker. Terrence doesn't play that way, he asserted to himself. Crouched in a duck walk he maneuvered between desks to the door. He kept expecting to hear sirens any minute, but none were audible yet. He made it to the door of the rear offices. No noise from within. "He's hiding like a cowering dog," Terrence mused to himself. "I wish I had time to enjoy this."

He turned the corner fast, unhesitatingly pointing his pistol out in front of him. It was a small secondary office with the Mayor's personal secretary's desks. "I heard you talking Larry. Get out from under those desks or I'll start shooting holes in them 'til red comes out from under one of them." No response. "Larry don't piss me off. I'm not a nice person when I'm angry."

"Neither am I." A voice came from the room to the rear of the secretary's office. The door was open to it. A large table took up most of the interior space.

"You better show some respect to me Mr. Mayor. I'm not in a mood to kiss your ass." Terrence walked slowly towards the door as would a cheetah stalking its pray in tall grass.

"You work for that Jew, Shoeghit, don't you?"

"Not any more, this is freelance now. I'm going to do you just for a trophy to add to my case. Come out where I can see you now."

"No, I can't do that."

"I heard you call the cops. You think I'm scared? You don't see me running do you?"

Terrence was almost at the door. The mayor's voice was louder with every step closer. He could feel the anxiety in his voice. "Step out and lay down on the floor Larry, I won't kill you. I just want to embarrass you a little. A cheap thrill. Come on, what could I do? You know the cops are coming. They should be here right now." The Mayor's feet stuck out into plain view, laying flat with his heels up.

"OK, do whatever disgusting thing you want."

"That's a good boy." Terrence walked into the room. It was the conference room, with a large desk in the middle and twelve chairs surrounding it. The mayor in his expensive suit was lying face down at the side of the entrance to it. After looking on the other side of the desk he approached the mayor and stood over him.

"What are you going to do, piss on me?"

"Ah if I only had to go. No it's payback time."

"Can I confess something first?"

"A death bed confession? Sure. Hurry though. I have a busy day ahead."

"I didn't actually call the cops."

"Is that it? You're going to try to pull one over on me now? You must think I'm an idiot."

"No just a sucker." The mayor rolled into Terrence's shins and lifted a pistol he had hidden under his belly to Terrence's groin, and fired point blank. Pow! The bullet went right up the inside of his spine like a guide-rail and sent blood and guts everywhere. Terrence fell on top of the mayor still breathing but not coherent. Larry pried the gun out of his hand and tossed it up onto the large table. Then he pushed and squirmed to get out from under Terrence. "Damn! You're a big nig."

Getting to his feet the mayor kicked Terrence in the head. Alive but unable to move Terrence moaned in pain. "He he he! You didn't know what you were messing with, did you? You must think they give this job to morality majors. Yahoo!" He kicked him again and again and again sadistically. Terrence's face swelled, dripping blood from the corners of his mouth and ears. It didn't stop the mayor though. He kicked and kicked 'til his foot finally hurt so bad he had to stop. Mayor Bennard tried to compose himself from the state of uncontrollable laughter. "Oh God, that was fun. If I could only do that more often."

The door opened at the back of the conference room, startling the mayor. Larry Bennard whirled around drawing the gun up at the figure entering.

"Don't shoot! It's me. Richard."

"What happened? Where did you run to?" He said after lowering the gun and looking at his prize catch lying on the floor dying.

Richard responded, his breathing labored,

"They kidnapped me from my home and forced me to let them in to the office, or they would have killed me, they said."

"So your solution was to turn them loose on me? That's ridiculous, I ought to fire you after the election for that. That's loyalty!"

"Well I knew security would be tight after, well, after your brother got killed."

"So open the locks and let them in was your answer? Then run off screaming like a girl, 'HELP, HELP?' Idiot."

"Well, it worked," Richard expounded, The assassins ran off. And we got one here. The cops will find the girl and the big Jew guy. By the way. Where are the cops?"

"I haven't called them yet."

"What!? Are you crazy? I thought they were here. That guy with the Uzi could still be out front."

"Let's go see." The mayor walked brazenly into the front reception area, gun down to his side. Richard followed slowly, not assured of his safety. "There's your big Jew," Larry exclaimed stopping in the middle of the room, pointing to the corpse, "and there's my two dead bodyguards blown to pieces, thanks to you. Now how do you feel about your plan? I know both of their families personally. I'm going to make you go with me to tell them, you idiot."

"Larry," Richard asserted strongly, "Think in terms of your career. Think in terms of the city, a million residents. These are just a few faceless people. This will win the election for you. You realize that, don't you?"

Mayor Bennard stood in the middle of the room like a statue, thinking quietly for a minute before responding. "Yes, but I'm still pissed off at you."

"Shoeghit caused this. If it hadn't happened here it would have gone down somewhere else. It's better they went after you here."

"How do you know Shoeghit's behind this?"

"They told me, the black guy and the girl. They were to kidnap me. Shoeghit had paid them to do it, but Shoeghit changed the deal, blackmailing them to kill you. They were aware that they were to be the patsies as well as the assassins. They asked me to run for it as soon as I got through the door and they would pursue me only to escape from Shoeghit's goons and disappear. I didn't follow the plan though because it would have left Shoeghit's soldier with a clear path to you, so I took a chance and yelled for all I could, then ran for cover. When they panicked, the girl ran down the hall so I chased, her but she escaped through the garage. Then I came back to see if you were alright. I assumed the police would be here by now."

"No I don't want the police yet," the Mayor insisted, "I don't want any survivors." He turned and walked back into the conference room stepping over Terrence on the floor and then turning to face him. Richard followed but stopped at the door way. "You know where my roots are from. Organized crime. I was just smart enough to legitimize myself before the authorities got wise. Shoeghit's finally overstepped himself this time. Is he still breathing?"

Richard bent down to his knees and reached out with his hand in front of Terrence's disfigured face, feeling for his breath. "I can't tell."

The Mayor took his pen out of his breast pocket and went to the table. The silenced pistol Terrence had had in his hand lay in the middle of it. He stuck the pen down the barrel and lifted it up without touching the surface of the metal. He then walked over to the body of Terrence where Richard was still kneeling by it. Grabbing Terrence's limp hand Larry wrapped it around the handle of the gun and guided the trigger finger into the slot. Then he held it up to Terrence's temple and leaned back as far as he could to avoid the splatter. Richard jumped up and stepped back a couple of steps.

POP! The gun fired into the side of Terrence's

head spilling his brains out the other side. Mayor Bennard grinned. "Well, there goes another one of my critics." He set the hand back down carefully on the floor. A pool of blood grew wider and wider from the head.

"Should we call the cops now?"

"In a minute. Let's get our stories straight." The mayor stood back up and turned away, stepping over to the table to piece together his alibi. "You realize I could have you arrested for conspiracy, or accessory, don't you?" Bennard vocalized in an menacing tone. "I can't believe you led those killers down here and let them in. I'm beginning to wonder if you're a friend or an enemy. Let me tell you what you're going to do for me. You are going to say exactly what I tell you to say to the media, when I tell you to. Got it? Or I'll have you added to the list of recently deceased, and I mean it. Always remember Richard, I'm a politician first, employer second, and a friend last. I don't take disloyalty from anyone. You're with me or against me, no middle ground."

The mayor turned around, hands on his hips, still fuming with his pissed off demeanor intending on reiterating his distaste for Richard's actions. His face wrenched into distorted surprised expressions when Richard wasn't standing in the doorway but was now kneeling down over Terrence's dead body, lifting the gun up, cupping his hand around Terrence's limp hand and aiming it at him.

"Don't move an inch, boss." Richard said sarcastically.

The mayor froze, stunned. "Richard, wait a minute. Don't misunderstand me. I'm not going to have you arrested. That's why I said we had to get our stories straight You're my chief of staff, I wouldn't fire you. Ever. We go back a long way, old friend."

"Oh yes you would, you tyrant. You would fire your mother if you thought it would further your career."

"Hey, Richard, it's just politics, I'm the mayor, I have..."

"Stop!" Richard interrupted. "You aren't the mayor anymore."

"What are you talking about, he can't win..."

"I'm the mayor." The brow curved up on Richard's face in a shrewdly evil angle, framed with a smile only a demon from hell could match.

Larry looked at him with fear in his eyes. He knew what he meant but was trying to act like this wasn't happening.

"As a parting thought, I want you to remember, I'm a politician first, employee second, and I never was your friend, you piece of shit." Pop, Pop, Pop. Richard pulled the trigger with Terrence's hand on it, emptying the rest of the bullets into the chest of Mayor Bennard. He lurched back, the table edge stopping him at the waist then curled over to the side and fell to the floor. Struggling for a second back to his knees he attempted to regain his feet and then fell flat to the floor only a foot from Terrence's body.

******

Noon Sunday. The warm sun shone through the long extended solar windows on the angled roof of Steve's loft. The first hours of sun for over five days in San Francisco's cold fall weather, it was to spell the city only temporarily as the dark black clouds waited at the horizon of the Pacific Ocean on their way with more cold winds and rain.

The loft normally neatly organized was strewn with tools, equipment being readied, dirty dishes, papers, and wet cloths all over it. Its frenzied inhabitants showed no regard to the future, feverishly trying to fix the present. Steve's television's surround-sound system replayed the booming shots of the events at the union hall. Like the shot heard 'round the world, Jack Swanson getting blown in half by the anarchist days before the election had had the same effect on the city. Gena sat motionless in front of the TV watching her ex-boyfriend on the video, captivated at the ugly deed, replaying it over and over again. Steve insisted on playing the video for her to give her an idea what she was dealing with. He wanted to be sure to wash out any thoughts she might have of Ivan still being innocent or framed.

At the same time Steve intensely attempted to decipher the letters that came out of the safe in the heist at Frank Ross's HQ. He had kept them in his car instead of turning them over to Terrence and Nova that day. He had literally forgotten about them, only saving them for amusing reading while on vacation. They had never been intended to be used. Now he was feverishly attempting to decode the letters at his computer desk in hopes they could find something to leverage against the people that pursued them.

Steve was good at puzzles. Most of them were financial records he had summarized rather fast, hidden debts to Shoeghit and other anonymous players to be paid back by once in office. They were hopelessly encrypted, waiting for a computer to decipher them when necessary.

There were two long letters unencoded, which had dirt on people and a list of addresses of apartment complexes Shoeghit owned. Each complex had one empty studio set up for off-the-record meetings. Each one could be a safe place to hide and needed to be checked out.

One letter was particularly juicy, and very useable. The chief of police Ken McHale had been accused of sexual harassment by his secretary who later quit. It said here that Bennard smoothed the whole thing over by promising her money and a job in the administration if she didn't go public and sue. It asked if she would let things cool off for a month. Then stapled to the back of the letter was an obituary of her demise in a car wreck with a drunk driver. How Frank Ross got his hands on it is even better. It was from Richard Morris the chief of staff for Bennard, asking to be kept on after the election if Mayor Bennard lost. Looks like old Richard's not happy with Larry Bennard. Shoeghit couldn't possibly have known about this letter or he would have asked for it back when he had me up in the Embarcadero Tower.

"That son of a bitch," Steve mumbled out loud. "Frank could have got his friend Shoeghit, money-backer/string-puller off the hook but he didn't. He just stood right there and let all these events unfold like he couldn't do anything to help. He probably wanted Shoeghit to go to jail."

Gena turned and looked at him for a second, but then returned her attention to the television.

Steve read on. The second letter wasn't as clear but used catch words and riddles. After some time it became apparent that this was a list of three addresses that could be used for meetings and/or safe houses for illicit activities. The mayor could go get some pussy, drink, do drugs, out of the public eye. Places to wheel and deal with the underworld.

Gena turned off the VCR and walked over and stood next to Steve at his desk. He didn't acknowledge her, keeping his head down focused on the letter. He was like a computer downloading a file into his permanent memory. This was information he must remember whether he had the paperwork on him or not. Vital tools of knowledge that could save himself and Gena. Like the old saying, "They can never take your education away," the same principle applied: they can't erase his memory.

"I can't believe he did that."

"Who," Steve replied.

"Ivan," Gena said, "I can't believe he shot that man."

"When you hang around a rough crowd, bad things will happen, that's guaranteed."

The phone rang on the wall in the kitchen. Steve lowered the paper he was reading but did not get up to answer. Gena stood behind him reaching up and massaging the trapezius muscles on his shoulders while he listened. The answering machine clicked on, silently running the recording then clicked again loudly playing the call being recorded.

The desperate voice of a girl came on the line. A voice Steve had thought he would never hear again. "Steve, Steve it's Nova. If you're there pick up, please! It's an emergency, please!"

Steve looked over his shoulder at Gena with a slightly stunned expression on his face. He had assumed Nova was dead from what Shoeghit had told him. He jumped up from his desk bolting across the floor of the loft to the kitchen, yanking the phone off its holder on the wall.

"Hello, hello, I'm here!"

"Steve I'm in trouble."

"Stop!" He fired back, his years of experience on the run taking control of the emotions from hearing her voice. "Where are you calling from?"

A three second pause went by before she responds. "A pay phone downtown."

"OK. Don't stay on the phone more than two minutes. I thought you were dead. They told me that they killed you."

"No," she said almost in tears, "Steve, I'm sorry about everything," her softness evident on the phone. He could barely make out her voice through the industrial receiver on the pay phone. The few downtown pay phones had all the delicate electronics of a war bunker. He could feel she was in desperate straits.

"They told me both of you were dead. What, what's going on? I don't understand. Where were you? Where did you go? Why didn't you call in? You know Shoeghit's been running around saying you were dead? What happened?"

Steve realized something was up. He was pretty sure Nova and Terrence had double crossed him, but this wasn't the time or the place to address that. If Nova wanted to come back, even for a little while, he could use her talents. Honor among thieves. Steve was starting to see himself acting like the very politicians he so despised. Working with people that had backstabbed him just days before. Using them for the moment and then getting rid of them after they'd lost their usefulness.

He argued within himself, "You're the Master Thief, you set the example, the code of honor. You will have honor and help Terrence and Nova even if not purely for the fact of looking at yourself in the mirror in the morning without guilt."

"He forced us, Steve. We had to do as he said, or he was going to kill us. He made us a deal that if we could get him close to the chief of staff, we could go, leave town and he wouldn't hold it against us for stealing his money. So we did what he said. Then when we delivered the chief of staff to him all tied up he double-crossed us on the deal."

Making deals with the devil. You sure you didn't hesitate to tell them to look for me down on Broadway Friday night, Steve reflected silently.

"They forced us down to the mayor's office, It's on the news now."

"What's on the news?"

"We had a gun-fight in city hall. I ran for my life. Steve," Nova's voice was shaky and scared. "I left Terrence behind. I'm pretty sure some cops got hurt. What do I do Steve? I'm scared."

"Have you watched the news?"

"No I've been running."

"Ok, Switch phones. Move a good distance and call me back in twenty minutes on my cell phone. I'm turning on the TV right now, let's see what's transpired. Gena, turn on the TV, channel six."

Nova didn't answer, the panicked thief hung up and fled as her old boss had instructed.

The big screen TV flashed on. Gena flipped through the channels 'til she arrived at channel six. The reporter for channel six, Jimmy Lanier, stood in front of City Hall immersed in a mass of people crushed up against police barricades which were being held up by police officers in riot gear. Behind the wall of cops a yellow tape was strung across the doors of City Hall marking the no entrance police investigation in progress.

Jimmy Lanier tried to report the news as he was jostled about by the excited crowd. He pushed his earpiece into his ear hard, trying to hear the reports trickling into the news room from a source calling in from inside the building.

"Apparently," Jimmy screamed into his microphone, "There has been a shooting in the Mayor's Office and some injuries have occurred, no...wait...stand by." He listened to his earpiece, people around him leaning in to hear what he was reporting. "Now apparently, according to a source inside, the mayor has been injured, and at least one man is dead."

The crowd moaned and whoa'ed with disbelief.

Gena grabbed hold of Steve, scared. "Ivan? did they kill Ivan? Is he the one that got killed?"

"I don't know. Listen," he hushed her up.

"Yes, we can confirm a shooting has just happened on the second floor of City Hall in the mayor's office. Early reports state that a group of three to four armed assassins entered through the back entrance used by employees, climbed the stairs to the second floor and penetrated the reception area of the mayor's office where they were met by the Mayor's security team. The two SFPD cops attempted to stop them and the gun battle ensued.

"We're still not sure how the mayor got hurt. Speculation indicates a stray bullet might have grazed him. The injuries don't appear to be significant due to the fact that he has not yet been transported to the hospital."

The reporter, Jimmy, paused for a minute as the camera panned around City Hall. The growing crowd of people increased rapidly. Hundreds of flickering red lights, strobed off the building's gray walls. The building stood powerfully, rising out of the crowd like a monolithic altar.

"Every plan I had just got fucked up again," Steve expounded in frustration. "God damn people!"

"Now what do we do?"

"Don't look at me, I don't know."

"Are we in more trouble again?"

Steve thought for a second before responding. "Actually no... Well, I'm not sure. We're on shaky ground. But, what else is new?"

The camera on the television shifted suddenly to the door as the police chief emerged from the building's front doors. He ducked under the yellow tape and walked down the stairs to the waiting cameras. The bright spot lights illuminated him dramatically as they circled around him at the barricade. A number of reporters anxiously screamed out questions, each progressively louder.

The Chief held up his hands, telling everyone to quiet down.

Gena and Steve looked on silently absorbing all the images.

"I have an announcement to make!" Chief Ken McHale said as loud as he could without yelling. The crowd hushed spontaneously to listen.

"At this time, and with deep emotion, I regret to announce that the Mayor of San Francisco, Larry Bennard, along with two police officers, were shot and killed in the mayor's office. They were confirmed dead from multiple bullet wounds by the paramedics fifteen minutes ago. Two assailants' bodies were also found in the same area. Reportedly one assassin got away. At this time the only description we have is a Latin woman, middle-aged with long black hair."

A few random moans bellowed out, followed by complete stunned silence.

"We'll set up a formal news conference in one hour at police headquarters. The entire City Hall has been declared a crime scene and is off-limits to anyone for the time being.

"Who's in charge now?" a reporter screamed out.

Starting to walk back, he realized he should answer that one last question. He stopped and quickly returned to the circular concave of reporters. "The Chief of Staff is the next in the chain of command. Richard Morris will be acting Mayor until the election."

"Are we still having the primary tomorrow?"

"No, I'm going to recommend an emergency session of the City Council to postpone the primary at least 'til Wednesday. Maybe longer. I have an investigation in progress so excuse me. We will answer all questions at the news conference." The chief waved his hand in a cutting-off motion and walked away back into the building.

News 6's camera man panned down to their reporter Jimmy Lanier struggling for some space shoulder to shoulder with a dozen other reporters, "We'll be moving over to the police station for roughly a three o'clock news conference on the events at City Hall . . ."

Clicking off the television with the remote, Steve set it down and walked over to the sofa. He sat down stroking his beard in thought. "Interesting, no doubt about it. Never in my wildest dreams would I have thought things would have gotten this out of hand."

The phone rang again, this time the cellular. Gena picked it up off the coffee table and handed it to Steve.

"Hello," he said casually as though nothing had happened."

"It's me," Nova responded.

"Well, did you see the news?"

"No."

"The mayor's dead."

No response. Steve could hear her breathing like she was going to hyperventilate.

"How many people did you enter with?"

"Me, Terrence, and that man that Shoeghit sent with us."

"Well Nova, it looks like you're the only survivor. Do you have any plans?"

"No," she said back frantically. "Can you help me?"

"There's not much I can do. All those lectures I gave you about laying low and sticking together must not have meant anything to you."

"Steve, I'm sorry. It's not my fault though. You would have done the same thing."

"Somehow I doubt that."

"Steve help me," Nova pleaded.

The wise old hawk had known what to do all along, but he wanted her to get scared and feel helpless so she would know who to depend on...Who her only true friend was.

"Didn't you say you had some family in South America? Don't say where over the phone. You just need to go there for now."

"But how Steve? I have no money. I can't go home!"

"OK, OK, I'll get you some money for a ticket. Then you leave 'til I say to come back, and that might never happen. You stay down there at least a year, then maybe we'll get you a new identity and you can come back and work for me. That's the deal. Not negotiable."

"Yes, yes I'll take it. I'll do anything you say."

"Get lost again, we'll meet at site number 5 of our emergency locales. Do you remember the emergency escape meeting areas? Five o'clock, be there." Steve clicked off the phone without waiting for her to answer.

Gena studied him sitting on the couch, "Well you seem relaxed?"

"I couldn't be more happy," he responded smiling. The tension had left his voice. His tone was of relief, like a big weight had been lifted off his shoulders.

Gena inquired, "Why so happy?"

"Why? Because Shoeghit was the one who had the gun to both our heads. Do his dirty work or die. Well the times they are a-changing. Now he's on the run. Watch, mark my words. He's a big fat fish in a pool of piranhas. Shoeghit's lost his power base, he's crippled politically. His contacts are distancing themselves from him as fast as they can, his candidate doesn't stand a chance in hell at winning. God, I love it! Now it's time to make my moves." Steve looked over at Gena, "Or, I mean our moves. The chaos plays well for us. I've got a set of plans we're going to execute. Pump down some caffeine, we're going to be busy."

7

Sunday afternoon 2:45pm. Touw had called Steve earlier on the cell phone and said he was going to do some leg work trying to round up information on Ivan. He couldn't sit still any longer waiting for Steve, so he re-outfitted the car with spikes and fueled it up. There was something he had been wanting to take care of on Haight Street for a long time, and it conveniently fit into the scheme of things this time. There was a bar where the hateful anarchist cliques would probably be. Rockers, bikers, generally the white trash's refuge if there was one in SF. Since they were on the run and all hell was breaking loose, he couldn't think of a better time to go pay a visit. "Who knows?" he told himself, "You might even find Ivan."

The Buick pulled down Haight circling around a couple of times. Amusingly the people here acted as though they knew nothing of what had happened on the news. They're all in their own little worlds, not conscious of anything but money-drugs-buzz, money-drugs-buzz. Worthless slaves, shackled by a substance. Idiots!

Touw had one particular place in mind. The bar had left a bad taste in his mouth a year ago and he was looking for revenge. His sister had been dragged down there on some pathetic sympathy date she didn't even want to go on, but she felt sorry for the guy. Her date ended up going to the Cool Rider here on Haight to parade her around like an accomplishment, to show he was worthy of their admiration and could be accepted as a Rocker amongst the fellows.

A bunch of fucking nerdy drunks with long hair, never been laid in their lives, relentlessly came on to her while her date stood by and watched frozen with fear to say anything in her defense.

Admittedly, Touw thought to himself as he parked the car, his family had a wild streak in it, but they were also very smart. They prided themselves on being intellectuals. She could have talked circles around anyone of the number of imbeciles frequenting that establishment. Eventually he had to come and pick her up that night due to the Rock and Roller's display of pathetic dating incompetence. The stud or pud that brought her was too busy male-bonding with his friends to take five minutes and drive her home. Yes, it was a personal vendetta he admitted to himself, but this was a perfect place to find Ivan. And if he got locked up for life or killed in the streets, he could smile knowing he had embarrassed these stupid people just one time.

Touw had a deceptive nature about him. Boyish looks but solid as a rock underneath his clothes. Muscle from head to toe and lightning fast. A small man 5' 5" 140lb on a good day, but armed with a temper only an Irishman could appreciate.

The big Buick barely squeezed into the tiny space among the sea of beat-up old seventies cars crammed into every inch of the Haight. Touw activated the alarm and started checking the area on foot. He circled around the Cool Rider bar a couple of times looking for any anarchist types. A number of Harleys framed the entrance of the bar as if to make a statement of the type of people that were inside. It was Sunday afternoon and it always drew a decent crowd of Rocker tough guys. Touw just laughed. They were about as dangerous as Mormons after church.

Touw could almost blend in well down here if he dressed for the part. His naturally black Asian hair had small red streaks tinted into it. He had innocent looks but a trash-mouth that had stunned more than a few people on occasion.

At the corners of the intersections there were a number of street kids stationed on panhandling patrol with their piercings and their dreadlock hair styles, looking for the money to get their fixes for the night. Touw quizzed them in short sporadic sentences. The kind of language they were used too.

"You seen Ivan? Ivan? Anybody seen Ivan?" Shoulder shrugs and confused looks abounded. Nobody seemed to know. "Enough of this, let's have some fun." Touw approached the Cool Rider bar's door with its red exterior and bubble-pane glass front window so no streeters could peer in. The stainless-steel sign was left unpainted hanging at an angle purposely to give a rough appearance. A man's man bar, no sissies. He walked in, the darkness from inside enveloping him, extinguishing even the minimal daylight from the overcast day.

It was a small bar, rectangular interior space heading back length wise from the door. The establishment was taken up mainly by the long bar with stools along it, with three cheap tables against the facing wall. A small space in the rear at the end of the bar was a pool table, with a couple of stools placed in the corners to sit on. At the very end of the bar past the pool table were stairs going up to a restroom. About ten rocker type men punctuated the establishment. Two groups of three were playing pool, and two groups of two were sitting at the bar drinking.

Touw laughed to himself disgusted by these people. You always saw them in groups of two or more, he mused. They're too much a bunch of pussies to come out on their own. Touw had a low-life persona also, he knew it, but he also had a degree of class to him. You can be poor and in the gutter, but be respected. The one thing they couldn't take from you was your pride, although they would try. When you let your self-respect go, then all you were was a needy clone, looking for acceptance from anyone you could get it from. Wanting to hang around people that were needy clones too and could understand the disgrace you felt about yourself. Misery loves company. "That's what all you fucks are," Touw said out loud as he stole in. He made it about four steps into the bar before the bartender bellowed out in a derogatory tone looking over his shoulder while cleaning a glass, "Hey! Stop right there!"

Touw stopped, acting as if surprised. He wasn't.

"Yeah, you slope head......I mean red head."

He looked over not giving him the courtesy of a smile like so many Asian passives did. He slowed his step and diverted to the edge of the bar. The two men at the bar three seats down were looking at each other laughing, entertained at the bartender's racist remark.

"This bar's 21 and over, you're not in Saigon." The bartender stood towering over Touw from behind the counter. He threw his chest out and shoulders back to add to the dissimilarity in sizes.

Touw reached in and pulled out his ID thrusting it into the bartender's face.

The bartender grabbed it out of his hand pulling it to his body sadistically stepping back out of Touw's reach. "Let me look carefully at this, you know you all look so much alike. This could be your brother, or......your sister." The two fans of the disgracing in progress burst out in laughter a degree louder that the last time. The attention of the other two rocker clones at the end of the bar near the pool table was now fixed on the unfolding scene as well.

Touw stood there rigid, his stare transfixed on the bartender's chin, not wanting to look him in the eyes yet. The anger was like coal in the furnace of his adrenalin stores. He was so alive at this moment. It dwarfed daily living, rudimentary bullshit day-to-day existence. A couple of seconds went by in the charade of an inspection.

"What's your birthday?"

Touw looked at him for a second, this time in the eyes, then told it to him softly, just audibly, "February twenty-fifth, seventy one."

"That's it," the bartender staring down at him handed the ID back, turned his back to him and walked away, not even asking him if he wanted a drink. The two long haired rocker boys smiled and looked down at their drinks about three stools down from Touw.

He looked over at them now, as they didn't return his gaze.

"Something funny?"

The two looked back at him, "No," brown haired mop sitting closest to Touw said. He then turned back to his friend and giggled like a little school girl would.

Touw reiterated to himself: man, fifteen of these wusses in here and they still won't stand up to a small Asian man. He walked over and sat next to the guy, uncomfortably close to the rockers. Only then did brown hair turn around and look directly at him.

"Hey! Don't get too close now!" the rocker said loud enough for the whole bar to hear. "Do you mind? We're talking here."

"That's funny. I didn't see you talking, just laughing. Can I hear the joke? I want to hear the joke." Touw leaned closer to them.

The guy's head rotated away from Touw to the other blond mop rocker on the stool next to him and a barely discernible "You are the joke," was spoken to him, followed by a wheezing laugh.

"Why don't you want to be my friend?" Touw asked, silencing the two idiots as they looked at him curiously.

The bartender came back down to the group.

He was used to drugged-out kids walking in off the Haight. He interjected himself into the conversation. "Do you want a drink, or what?" he said pointedly at Touw.

"Ah...yes," Touw replied diplomatically, "You turned and walked away from me so I assumed you didn't want to give me one."

"What do you want!" The bartender fired back, irritated.

"A shot of XO. That's cognac if you don't know what that is. Do you have that in this...place?" Touw asked derogatorily.

"Those are fifteen dollars a shot. You got it?"

Pulling out a roll of money an inch thick from his pocket, he peels off a hundred from the top, "Make it two then."

The scruffy older, flat topped, bow-tie bartender, turned around and dug out a dusty bottle from under the bar in a cabinet reserved for the good booze. He poured out two shots to the amusement of the cheap-assed rockers sitting next to Touw. Touw turned his attention to them. "So what's so funny with me? You don't like me in here?"

The bartender interrupted, "Hey, come on now. Let's not go there."

"Go there? You've been going there the entire time I've been here. You just don't want me to go there. Right?"

The bartender put down the bottle after only filing half the first shot. "All right kid, I've had about enough from you."

"Enough of WHAT, you hypocrite? Walk in here and get treated like shit and you expect me to smile?"

The two long hair rockers turned and looked at him, studying him carefully. He looked back. "FUCK YOU! You guys are pieces of shit!" he said pointedly at them.

The two picked their beers up off the bar and walked down to the end of the bar not saying anything back and sat with the other two long haired rockers. Touw just sat in amazement at how spineless they were. "What do you have to do to start a fight in here?" he thought to himself. If this were a Vietnamese bar it would have been turned upside down by now. What happened to all the tough-guy-badged warriors that walked around here? I guess they needed reinforcements. He watched them. They were all talking amongst themselves, pumping each other up for the big event. Leaning against the bar like John Wayne he drank the half shot of cognac, and looked at the bartender.

The wise coward behind the bar realized Touw wasn't going to budge one inch without a fight and poured him another drink, "That one's on me," he said nicely. "Just take it easy sport.

What's on your mind, come in to watch football?"

"Yes, as a matter of fact, I did. Me and my friend Ivan, have you seen him? You know him, Ivan the terrible."

The bartender leaned over the counter. "He's not here," he said softly. "He's in a bunch of trouble, I doubt he'll be down. Is that the reason or do you need some sniff? I can hook you up."

"No, just need to talk to him. I have some information he needs for getting out of the trouble he's in. Little details he needs to know about his case." Touw looked in the mirror behind the counter while talking to the bartender. The mirrors in that position are an old tradition. They're there to prevent patrons from steeling tips or alcohol when the bartender's back is turned. They can be used in another way as well. Touw could watch the entire bar including the end where the rockers were and not have to turn his head.

The group of rock-and-roll cowards with their girls hairdos had pumped themselves up with enough buddy-buddy tough guy talk to play their hand. Two of them were slowly walking down to Touw, their steps hesitant, not confident. They looked more scared than angry. Touw squared his shoulders to them, standing away from the bar. He took the shot off the counter and shot the whole thing down.

The bartender stopped talking. He observed the rockers but did nothing to stop them. The long haired rockers stopped for a moment just out of swinging range of Touw. It was like they didn't know what to say.

"You going to stand there all day?"

"We don't like the way you talked to us," the blond one asserted.

"Why don't you do something about it, pussy? Fucking pussies. Look at you, you look like fucking girls. Girly hairdos, faggots!"

Both of them scowled their faces into fighting expressions, but still they were frozen in their tracks, like their legs were bolted down to the floor.

Touw stood his ground dumbfounded. But the action never came. "Come on let's do it!"

The brown haired one shook his head, "No, no." He turned around and walked off holding his hand up in a stopping gesture. The blond followed him walking away as well shaking his head as if he was better than to belittle himself. They chuckled like they had played a prank.

Touw yelled loud so the entire bar can hear, "What do you mean, no?"

"You're not worth the trouble."

"I'm not worth the trouble?" Touw took the empty shot glass off the bar and hurled it at them with the velocity of a baseball pitch, beaning one in the head. The shot-glass ricocheted off his head and bounced across the pool table. The blond haired rocker grabbed his mound of hair massaging his skull. The flaky friends of the four at the end of the bar playing pool laughed at their acquaintance's predicament. "There. Now am I worth the trouble?"

Finally one had had enough. As the blood from the skull of the blond guy tainted his pretty hair red a third one with medium length black hair sitting at the end of the bar charged.

He sprinted flat out at Touw in a parallel line to the bar. Two more of the four joined right behind him, fists clenched angrily snarling like wild dogs. The bartender stood motionless only folding his arms across his chest in a judgmental position, as if to say you asked for it.

Touw raised to the toes of his feet, spreading his legs slightly wider. The first attacker in a bull rush like a fullback trying to run over a linebacker entered his strike zone. He spun a round-house kick from as far back as he could reach cracking the black haired rocker in the temple and diverting his momentum to the ledge of the bar. He crashed through the bar stools toppling to the ground, stools bouncing across the floor. Without even stopping his move Touw continued his motion at the second attacker, testimony to his ten years of Martial Arts training. His second strike was a driving elbow to the next oncoming rocker hitting him in the face. The rocker's flailing hands failed to hit Touw's head. He ducked and bobbed reestablishing his balance, then followed through with a upward double hand bench press style move again into the guy's face toppling him backwards, while the third one piled into him. Lifting his knee to his chest, he drove his strong leg down into the back of his neck, wrenching his head and throwing his torso down as you would experience in a car accident. He crashed to the floor, his face embedding into the filthy tiles. The third attacker who stumbled back falling to his butt was trying to get back up, but Touw with no sympathy eye-gouged him with one finger drilling it into the socket deeply, stunning him and then kneeing the guy viciously hard in the head, giving him ten times more than he bargained for. He collapsed to the floor whimpering.

Touw stood proudly in the middle of the victims of his wrath, like a hunter over his kill. His stare challenged any more opponents, but there were no takers. He stood in defiance of the cowards. The three rockers intent on rat-packing the smaller Asian opponent adorned his feet as symbols of ignorance and stupidity.

The bartender now made his play. He reached

under the cash register and pulled out a baseball bat. Touw didn't flinch, towering over his cowering captives who were too scared to get up. The six rockers that were playing pool all watched as a neutral audience, not helping or commenting in any way. The blond rocker bleeding from the head coaxed them to help his friends but no one stepped up.

Making a couple of sweeps across the top of the bar with the bat, the bartender made his intentions known. Touw just smiled.

"You've been standing there with your finger up your ass the whole time while I was to be rat packed. And now you get out the bat? Why didn't you get out the bat to stop these three?" Touw lectured him. "Why didn't you stop them from starting shit in the first place?" He hardened his stare, "I ought to kill you right now!"

The bartenders eyes widened inadvertently. He had let this situation get out of control and it was going to cost him. "Leave us alone damn it," he said scared, "I'm going to call the police."

Giggling, Touw repeated the same motion the rockers had insulted him with by waving his hand off. "Ah, you're not worth the time." He walked out stepping deliberately on a rocker's back before leaving.

******

One night there had been a show on the

Discovery Channel about the Navy Seals that Steve had watched. They had interviewed a Chief Petty Officer about what happens when things go wrong in a fight. The old Chief had just said simply, we run for the water. The water is our friend and protector. No military force can easily follow us there. They can't follow us at all.

Well, Steve wasn't much for swimming, but the idea was sound. Where could a thief go when he's in trouble? To the air. The last place in the world you would look for him. The SF police were ill equipped for that scenario.

Expensive toys—the master thief had tried hard to stay away from their allure. Idle time on your hands made for easy spending. Expensive cars with high insurance payments, maintenance bills. Clothes with three-figure price tags you only wore once and threw in the closet. He had to resist. That forced him to work when the situations were sketchy. He did allow one splurge though. A big pleasure, he had realized that it was always his dream to have one. Live your dreams if you can, he told himself. For years he had been all around his dream of flight, but it wasn't his to be had anytime he wanted.

Helicopters were his passion. In the military he had managed flight school and lived two years of heaven flying a Huey in Germany before his infamous transfer to Army Intel, then to the CIA.

When he finally got going again after the escape from his death warrant, he made it a point to get a set of wings no matter what he had to do.

Steve started shopping immediately for his own helicopter. It made total sense to him. He could use it for work or play. It was the ultimate escape vehicle. The local police were not tasked with equipment to counter a fully fueled chopper. He could fly anywhere, disappearing over the horizon at tree-top level, unrestrained by the need for a runway to land on. Radar could not track a low flying helo, that's why the army loved them.

Steve had wanted to make any part of the country accessible without having to stop at an airport. A number of craftily hid fuel drops with drums of JP5 Jet fuel for the turboshafts were buried underground already. The locations were programmed into the memory of his satellite navigation system in his helicopter. He intended to have them in hundreds of places across the country so he could jump around without being seen at an airport.

It seemed obsessive to him at the time but he reasoned that he needed the resources that his hunter would have access too. It was like a game: see how totally wired in you can get. Extreme deeds required extreme measures.

Steve had gotten as far as the lower half of the United States. He could jump into Mexico at several points along the border with a full load of fuel as far as Texas. With the helicopter he could land anywhere, steal a car and disappear forever.

He could also use his 'copter for surveillance. The SF cops weren't using helos because they were cheap. The large city police departments used them because they're undefeatable by someone on the ground. They were also virtually undetectable at night for surveillance. As long as you flew off the target far enough they never knew where you were. From the air you could see for miles. No one knew what you were doing. Sight-seeing is the assumption.

In the high stakes game Steve played, you needed the best equipment. A top of the line 'copter was needed, dependable, quiet and fast. Not too exotic, preferably one like the air ambulances used. Could be a good cover in a pinch.

The Aerospatiale Eurocopter was what three of the four flight-for-life outfits were using. Steve priced them, they were reasonable alright, but in his limited patriotism he didn't like the way the Euro boys set up their controls.

A brand new Bell Ranger was right within his price range but a little light for him. Something a bit nicer. Something an executive would jump from city to city in. Something that the law enforcement community wouldn't even dream a thief would be tooling around in.

He found what he was looking for but he had to get a small loan to purchase it. It was love at first sight. After a hacker fixed his credit report nicely for him at a price, he got his loan and acquired a McDonnell Douglas MD Explorer. State of the art fast and light. It was parked out at Oakland airport fueled and ready to go on a moment's notice. SFO was closer, but there was too much security snooping around. Oakland Airport police were a small force, badly undermanned. They had their hands full handling the punks at the metal detector.

The helicopter was a work of art and practicality. Five blade rotor for smooth lift and responsive turning, and no tail rotor to get bent by an accidental scrape with the ground. Ducted jet exhaust to counter-balance the rotation of the 'copter's blades. Room for six passengers to sit comfortably in a pressurized cabin. Three-hundred- and-fifty mile range at two-hundred miles an hour. Steve was able to add a hundred miles to the range by adding an internal fuel bladder. He also boosted the avionics with a satellite navigation system and autopilot options. In a bank above his head were mounted a number of sophisticated scanners and radio direction finders for his thieving work.

A thieving tool with no match. He could sit in

his helo late at night high up in the darkness with the quiet craft, set the autopilot and peer down with binoculars while listening to his scanners for shady conversations. He used this several times to locate drug-dealers' houses, their stealth fortresses where they stored their cash. To mark the address he simply counted the houses from the corner of the street then swooped by and read the street sign.

This procedure was used on one of his all-time favorite heists he committed four months ago. He had methodically traced the organization of a drug dealer's operation all the way up to the head man. He began with the crack dealers over in Oakland and worked up the food chain. He flew over them late at night and waited for their drop-man to come by. Sure enough, a big Cad pulled up and the boys piled in and circled the block then redeposited the bad boys back on the corner. The Cadillac then proceeded across town making several other stops before ending up pulling into a garage in Richmond and not reappearing.

The next day while they were sleeping Steve placed the bugs in the phone box at the end of the street and cased the place carefully from the ground.

After some hurried rest and recuperation he was up again over the house the next night. His directional antenna zeroed square on the roof with scanners looking for any calls over any wireless phone conversations. A different scanner was tuned to the bug placed on the land-line and recording all outgoing calls, which he monitored in real time. Within a couple of hours the big fish made himself known. No mention of drugs was made but a gray Toyota appeared, stayed for a moment and then calmly drove off toward the lights of San Francisco's Marina district. Steve found it amusing that the kingpin's main man was right in the middle of yuppy heaven. He probably went out and had coffee each morning with the ultra liberal goody goodies while infesting their streets with white poison. His cross-hairs had found the mark.

A simple burglary of the unsuspecting apartment had netted Steve a cool seventy five thousand in unmarked bills while the gangsters were away at the gym. I wouldn't have wanted to be in that guy's shoes when he had to explain where the money went for the dope, Steve daydreamed.

Thanks to the Colombian drug lords his helicopter was almost paid off.

Steve loved flying. It was his passion. A chance to remove yourself from the world and disappear into the sky. It was one of the contributing factors to keeping him sane in an insane world. No greater buzz could be achieved then to blast flat out through the two towers of the Golden Gate Bridge singing to AC/DC at the top of your lungs. Then at two hundred miles an hour bank off to the left and cruise down the coast shadowing Highway 1 with no particular place you were going and no particular time to be back, limited only by the amount of fuel you had.

On a nice day there was always a pretty girl in a convertible driving the windy road. Steve would drop down over her, smile and wave. Blow her a kiss and then move on. Women loved this and would always at least smile and wave back. If the response was extremely enthusiastic, Steve knew several places to set down and wait for the car to drive past. He would offer her a ride, and then fly out to the Farallon Islands just off SF and give them a different sort of ride. "Yes," he mused, the helicopter has its many advantages.

En route to Oakland he stopped at a grocery store to pick up some provisions with Gena. In case things took a bad turn, they might just set out for Mexico tonight. From the loft he brought a satchel full of money, about twenty pounds of cash, he had no idea how much, a camera-sized television and a number of weapons. The idea wasn't to pack-rat the limited space on board but not to be caught empty-handed either.

Steve really didn't want to start all over again.

He was more focused on fixing the current situation. If he had to run though, he could survive. When you own a helicopter south of the border, making money is never that hard. Smuggling in drugs wasn't what he wanted to be doing, though, for the rest of his life. In that trade you never left the organization alive. This was the world of the Listener Thief. Passively reacting to the situations as they happened around you. A rowboat in a strong tide. He could only do so much, row against the tide so long.

Gena had never flown in a helicopter and was anxiously anticipating her first flight. It would be nice to have a second set of eyes on board, Steve admitted to himself. He would have never fathomed bringing someone along with him, giving away his intelligence gathering methods. He didn't even bring any of his team with him, ever. That had always been his little secret...his mysterious way of getting the goods. Gena was different though. He thought of her as neutral. Criminally illiterate. In up to her neck with piranhas. No friends could help her, only Steve and his talents. Yes, he would enjoy her company.

The whine of the turbos screamed out as they came to life above the cockpit in the helo. The needle in the instrument gauges bounced and jumped across the console waking the

McDonnell Douglas Explorer from her sleep.

Gena buckled herself into the red and black cloth seat snugging down the safety harnesses and pulling the door shut. Steve reached across her to double check that it seated properly, then hit the rotor engagement lever starting the halo of blades spinning. The transfer case energized three green lights as power crested operating speeds for flight. He slammed his door then symbolically put his pilot's sunglasses on.

A light goose to the throttle caused the frame to creak from the lifting of the weight to the blades of the rotor. Almost unnoticeably, after that the two skids lifted from the ground as Gena looked out the bubble window in fascination. The Explorer climbed into the sky. Watching the airspace around him carefully, Steve, about a hundred feet up, tilted the nose down throttling up even more power out of the Pratt and Whitney turbines and aimed for The City. He leveled her out at three thousand feet and a hundred and fifty miles an hour.

Steve flew the copter effortlessly like it was an extension of his body. It was his utopia up here in the sky. The two chatted calmly, Steve showing her all the different gadgets in the cockpit.

"It's three o'clock Gena, time for the news conference. Would you be so kind as to get the

TV out?"

Gena nodded, undoing her seat belt to reach back into the cargo area and get it from the stores. She produced the small TV, turning it on to channel 6 and fine tuning the frequency in.

After checking the sky ahead of him, Steve set the autopilot so he could watch along with Gena. The tiny speaker, barely audible, came alive with the sounds of the crowd in the packed news room observing the swearing in of the new mayor.

Behind the podium a priest removed a Bible from Richard Morris's hand as a hundred flashes lit the room intensely. The reporter and witnesses clapped guardedly as though feeling that such an event requires some response. Richard Morris turned to the microphone to face the press for the first time as mayor. He seemed comfortable facing the sea of cameras and lights.

"I have very little good news to report to you. Becoming mayor in this manner is not an easy responsibility. However, in this time of crisis someone's got to step up and get this city back under control. I was very happy as chief of staff of this City of San Francisco. I will shoulder the duties of the mayor until after the election and will help with the greatest enthusiasm in assisting whoever wins the election in a smooth transition.

"I am deeply concerned however about the political implications of the last couple of days.

These events are not acceptable. We will not allow this government to stoop to the level of the behavior you see in some undeveloped countries. These are treasonous acts. The source of this violence must be dwelt with immediately, and with exacting justice. I stand before you this day, not in the mayor's capacity, but as a citizen of San Francisco, a witness to the unspeakable crime that happened in the office of the mayor. I witnessed Bill Shoeghit and his goons murder your incumbent mayor with my own eyes." The room of reporters gasped. "Yes! Frank Ross's string-puller. Come on people. Everyone in here knows this is so. It is Shoeghit with blood on his hands!" Richard blared into the microphone. "Bill Shoeghit was in the room at the time of the shooting, I saw him! The evidence is undeniable people: one of his bodyguards didn't make it out. His body was left at the scene, along with the hitman they hired. Two murderers dead. Two cops dead. The SFPD security team gave their lives in a desperate attempt to save the mayor. They paid the ultimate price trying to protect the mayor from this criminal Shoeghit. Out-numbered and out-armed they were gunned down unmercifully."

Richard Morris paused for a minute to look the captivated room over. He knew the story was being bought lock, stock, and barrel. He shook his head to show disgust while a few random camera flashes captured the moment for posterity. Very little noise came back from the room as the silence spoke volumes to the normally unruly reporters.

Richard attacked the microphone again, "I cannot stand by after watching the mayor, his brother, and two fine police officers get murdered for the right to take the power of the office of the city. We do not cower before the threat of violence. Letting Frank Ross and his criminal friends rape and pillage the great City of San Francisco. I will not stand for this. I will lend all my energy to preventing this. It's time for someone to step up! Therefore in these times of crisis I will take the place of the incumbent Mayor Larry Bennard and assume his candidacy in the mayor's race. Also, I have asked for, and received, an emergency session of the City Council to delay the election until this coming Friday, due to the extenuating circumstances."

Pausing once more to take a breath, Richard wiped the sweat from his forehead. "Also, if things weren't bad enough already, I have to report that less than thirty minutes ago at SF General, Jack Swanson the political consultant for Frank Ross, who was shot under questionable circumstances behind Bill Shoeghit's union headquarters, died from his wounds."

The crowd gasped one more time in disbelief.

"His last words to an aide were that he was sorry for ever getting involved with the Frank Ross campaign, and that something must be done to stop Bill Shoeghit. Another casualty of this nightmare. Chief Ken McHale will take the podium next and brief you about the on-going manhunt for Bill Shoeghit."

Steve reached over to the tiny knob on the television and turned it off. "Enough of that," he announced to Gena. She looked up at him, confusion in her eyes. Steve reached over and patted her on the thigh, "Don't worry, honey, you're in good hands this time."

8

Steve and Gena quickly sliced across the city with scary precision in the helicopter. Steve was curious if Shoeghit would show at one of the safe houses he had used throughout the campaign. Steve had all the addresses with him from the information removed from Frank Ross's safe. He prayed for Shoeghit to pop up at one of the secret locations out of the public eye. That would play right into his hands.

They spent a half hour flying above the various sites scanning for any phone conversations out of the area that sounded like Shoeghit's voice. Foot traffic was also of key interest: any suspicious person moving hurriedly, or even better loading packages. They darted from one to the other location repeatedly. It only took minutes due to the city being only forty nine square miles. They could usually watch two locations from the same spot high above.

Their surveillance was quickly coming to an end as the Pacific wind was blowing in off the ocean, stirring the fog up off Twin Peaks. They were having to fly too low, and it made the rotor sweep noise noticeable. Altitude was key to their anonymity.

Steve picked up the cellular phone from its fishnet holder on the front of the seat and dialed Touw in the ground vehicle, or war car, as they enjoyed calling it.

"Hey. Where are you at?" Steve asked casually.

"On my way out of the Haight."

"Did you catch the news conference? It was most intriguing."

"No, I'm afraid I didn't," Touw replied, "Had to check into something."

Steve thought for a second trying to figure what Touw was hinting, then went on. "OK," he replied sarcastically, "Nova's meeting us in the Japantown garage. We got some money for her to get to Mexico with."

There was a distinct pause before Touw responded to Steve on the phone, "And the time of this is?" Touw's voice was soft and guarded.

"Five o'clock sharp. I want you there, because she's supposed to be waiting there."

"And what was the garage again?" Touw queried back.

"J-town, the garage that links to the Miokai Hotel. Their hotel tower has a helicopter pad. I won't set down on it, though, I'll just drop it to you up there. Take it, go to her, give it to her and tell her to get the fuck out of our lives."

"A little harsh don't you think?"

"She's a double-crossing bitch, no honor in her blood, only greed."

"We knew that going in, Boss."

"Yes, well now I've decided she is not a friend anymore."

"That's good enough for me."

"You got ten minutes to be there. Let's make it happen." Steve grumbled into the phone.

Touw fired right back confidently, "I'm five minutes away."

Steve peered down out of the bubble window of the cockpit. He noticed the familiar Buick whipping a left off of Haight and shooting up Steiner Street. The huge hill in front of the famous painted ladies Victorians continuously besieged by tourists was like a launching ramp for the Buick. The suspension extended its full length cresting the top of the hill and plummeting down slamming the ground causing sparks to fly out. Touw must be doing eighty miles an hour Steve calculated. He passed Geary fish-tailing into a right and accelerating up

Post into the bowels of Japantown.

Gena was basically lost as to what was going on, more interested in taking in the views of the city from the high vantage point of the helicopter. That was fine with Steve, he didn't need to be bothered with frivolous questions right now. He was savoring the buzz of the energy of sweet revenge.

Do unto others as they do to you. Honor among thieves? Sell me out will you? He had decided to flip-flop on the do-good plan. Law of the jungle was in effect. If the female lioness does not stick up for the pride, she is ousted and left for the hyenas to eat. That's the way nature handled it. In doing so the hyenas got fed, and the pride got rid of dead-weight. It's that simple, he told himself.

He had given Nova his trust and had showed her what he knew. She had been treated with respect, and was trusted with information that could have put Steve in jail for the rest of his life. Now she had sold out, plain and simple. People were creatures of habit: Nova could no longer be trusted.

He banked the helicopter into a slow turn circling the tower of the hotel from two hundred feet above. In the war car Touw had just ducked into an adjacent garage.

Steve wrenched the stick back on the controls, lifting the helicopter up into the cloud cover. After leveling it out, he engaged the auto pilot and reached for a notepad in the pocket on the door. Writing a note to Touw on his thigh he stuck it in an envelope and then reached back and grabbed three thousand dollar bundles of hundreds out of the satchel and placed them in the sack as well. He looked at Gena, smiling and gave her a confident wink.

"So she's going to go to Mexico?" Gena inquired.

Steve smiled, "Yes she's going to Mexico, hon, got to get her someplace safe."

After completing the chore Steve removed the autopilot and ducked the nose of the helicopter once more, similar to an attack dive, circling left in a hundred and eighty degrees back. He headed straight for the high-rise tower at close to a hundred miles an hour air speed. He swooped down to the pavement just as the door to the roof opened with Touw emerging from it. The 'copter descended like an eagle after its prey pulling up only at the last second. Steve dropped the sack out his small vent window and then flew off across the skyline in order not to draw attention to himself. Touw retrieved it and darted back into the door, going to the roof and bolting down the stairs.

Throttling the full power of the turbines up, the two disappeared into the clouds for a moment circling the city using his satellite navigation system before returning at a high altitude and waiting up in the sky.

Peeking out the steel door as he shut it, Touw watched the helicopter disappear. He pulled the door to its jam and removed the alarm bypass. Calmly Touw walked down the hall of the top floor penthouse suites while fumbling with the envelope trying to open it. It was just another day on the job to Touw. He activated the elevator's down button while looking at the money he had dug out in his hands. Cash felt so good in his hands, like no other feeling in the world. As he flicked the corners like you would a new deck of cards a small slip of paper fell to the ground. He tucked the money into his coat pocket while leaning over and retrieving the note, as the elevator door opened in unison with the polite chime.

The watch on his wrist said five on the dot. He mashed the basement button and held the note up where he could see it. The scratchy writing on it said one sentence, "Nova's the bait."

He had known that before he read the note. The minute his boss had given out the location over the cell-phone, he had realized it was on. Then the time of the drop as well. It was like calling your opponent out for a fight in the old days of the schoolyard. A master thief would never make such a grievous violation of the code of conduct without a reason. Add the fact that Nova had screwed Steve over...well, it was the next logical move.

Shoeghit might be savvy enough to recognize the trap. But Touw knew mercenaries, and they sent their henchmen in first, usually. Especially since Shoeghit was probably going to flee prosecution. He'd want to mop up as best he could before leaving. It was refreshing to Touw to see his boss stepping up a level in the blood-thirsty underworld. He had always felt that that was his Achilles' heel, being too soft on his competition.

The elevator kept descending the length of the tower, dropping lower and lower. It was as if he were descending into the cauldrons of hell. The hair on the back of

Touw's neck was standing up. This was living. He stuck his hand on the grip of the MAC10 he had stuffed under his right shoulder and kept it there so it could be drawn instantly. The Berretta 9mm tucked into the small of his back at the belt and the Smith and Wesson .38 bull dog holstered to his calf, plus the long leather coat made Touw twenty pounds heavier than normal.

Stepping into the pit, maybe nothing will happen. Maybe Shoeghit's fled already. Nova will get her money and fly down to Mexico and live happily ever after. Touw didn't take the time to get attached to Terrence or Nova, so he was rather neutral on what would transpire. Not that he hadn't liked them or anything, but it was like being in a front line infantry squad in a war. Your buddies come and go in the underworld. Best to keep things casual, no personal attachments. This time it was paying off.

The elevator doors peeled back to the dungeon atmosphere of the parking garage. The cement walls and exposed pipes gave it a medieval feeling. The different colored cars were the only gems of aura in the space as Touw stepped cautiously, studying the area around him. About six different couples were moving either to or away from their cars. Touw started walking down the middle row of the three like a point man on a patrolling unit in the jungle, every movement caught his eye. He was unconcerned about drawing attention to himself reasoning that all hell was going to break loose momentarily, so what was the point in being clandestine. Besides, he reasoned to himself, these dumb-ass gang bangers walked around like this all the time anyway.

One hundred. Two hundred, Three hundred feet into the garage before a soft voice caught his attention. A noise with no face to it, emerging from a group of cars. "Psst." Touw turned and approached the block of six cars that spoke to him.

"Touw, come here. Over here."

Still with his hand in his leather coat gripping the butt of the MAC10, he was live as a glass bottle of nitroglycerin, ready to explode instantaneously. Step by painstaking step he eased up on the cars. Carefully Nova peeked up over the dash of a maroon Saturn on the back side of the row of cars that were parked nose to nose.

He adjusted his step and approached the driver's side window of the Saturn.

"Get in," Nova encouraged Touw.

"No I'd rather not," he replied coldly. Touw knelt to the side of the car. As she rolled down the window he studied her. She was not well. Her eyes showed wrinkles of extreme stress. Her normally long beautiful hair was knotted and matted. She had donned some lime-green sweats that looked like they had come from a Mission Street flea market. It wasn't the Nova he was used to.

As Touw knelt he pivoted back and forth on the balls of his feet to the right and to the left keeping an eye on all the people going about their business. One couple walked by looking at them, studying them curiously, but they were no threat.

"Do you have the money?" Nova quizzed him.

Taking his hand off the handle of the MAC10 only for a second he reached into his pocket and removed the three bundles of hundreds and handed them to her.

"Thank you Touw," she squeezed his hand in a assuring manner. "Where's Steve, is he outside?"

"He's around."

"I need help Touw, there's somebody watching me at the exit. I'm pretty sure. I'd feel better if someone could stand by 'til I left."

Touw nodded, not responding verbally.

"Some guy, up at the exit. He doesn't fit in."

"Are you sure about this?"

"Yes. Squinty eyes, a pock-marked face. He's just standing there. No reason. Dressed like a tourist, cheap slacks and a golf shirt."

"I think you're just paranoid, Nova," Touw questioned her stability. Inside he knew she was probably right.

"No, I'm sure of it, there's people at the other exits too."

"You're probably over-reacting, but I'll go check it out. No one knows you're here? Give me a minute to check it out, I'll walk up and stand by the door 'til you clear the exit."

"Thank you Touw," she said graciously, but sincerely.

He got to his feet and walked briskly down the middle aisle of the garage. He was now free of the exchange and more able to move around. Avoiding the confines of the stairs he preferred to stay out in the open. Touw walked up the automobile ramp to the top floor ignoring the signs that said "No Pedestrians." He knew trouble was waiting above. Walking directly up the middle of the ramp it was like announcing the showdown was about to begin.

Cresting the top of the ramp Roddy came into view standing stoically at the side of the exit booth. A seasoned vet of two real wars in Israel and countless encounters in the underworld he would back down from no one. Not today, or ever.

Touw walked up defiantly approaching to within twenty feet before stopping and backing up against the cement wall. His stare never left Roddy's hands, his peripheral vision sensitized to any unusual movement.

Within seconds the maroon Saturn appeared driving up the ramp very fast. Nova approached the exit, just barely in control from spinning out but had to stop from running through the gate because a lady in a Ford Explorer was getting money out of her purse at the booth. She couldn't run the gate. She had to stop. The anti-lock brakes strained to bring the car to a halt. Tensions skyrocketed as Touw's eyes blinked from car to Roddy and back to the car repeatedly.

Tension was like a lethal haze building from the area as oblivious shoppers and tourists walked back and forth. A woman broke from a group of people walking behind the Saturn and closed on Nova in her blind spot along the side of the car.

Touw's pulse raced, his face went flush.

The attendant handed the lady her change as the gate lifted, but she turned and asked for a receipt.

"SHIT!" Touw screamed, unable to hold it in. "Look out!" he yelled panicked at Nova, surprising himself. He looked at the car and then looked back at Roddy who was going for his gun in his shoulder holster.

A woman out of nowhere made it to the window of the car and reached into her shopping bag and removed a brick, then smashed the window.

Nova's head wrenched left, away from watching the booth, startled.

The lady reached back into the bag before dropping it to the ground and grabbed a foot-long double-edged knife driving it into the passenger area, trying to cut Nova's throat. She thrust it repeatedly, missing, horribly hitting Nova in the soft skin of her cheek ripping through both sides of her mouth and out the other side of her face. The muffled, garbled scream of the bloody mouth could be heard coming from the driver's window.

Elena, Shoeghit's hit-woman, reached back and thrust again into the torso of Nova, the steel digging deep to the bone. With her free hand Elena clawed a hold of Nova's hair, pulling her head closer to the window. Nova braced against the car door to keep from being pulled out of the window when Elena drove the large knife into her throat in a punching manner and then sawed back through it. Desperately Nova mashed the gas causing the Saturn to lurch forward ramming the Explorer and running right up under the bumper, the front wheels spinning and smoking. Glass and plastic flew everywhere as the head of the lady asking for the receipt cracked against the door-frame.

Elena never let go the whole time, stabbing and slashing at her face. The half a second distraction jeopardized Touw, for when he looked back at Roddy, Roddy had already cleared leather with his pistol and was raising it toward him. With Touw's small stature and lighting reflexes he jumped into the air, drawing the MAC10 at the same time. He let himself fall flat to his belly without attempting to break his fall.

Roddy, the old mercenary from Israel, tried to draw a bead on him. Bam! Bam!

Roddy capped off two rounds. The puffs of cement dust and sparks to the side of Touw indicated the misses.

Touw squeezed the trigger down as the MAC10 bucked and kicked, discharging its thirty rounds of destruction. It mowed down everything in front of him in a second's time. The undiscriminating weapon nailed Roddy four times, lifting him up onto his toes like a rag doll and then over onto his back. As Roddy fell Touw squinted in disgust with himself, looking at three more bodies behind him crumbling to the ground. One lay motionless, face down, to the side of the toll box. A man holding his gut struggled to his feet and heroically dove over his injured girlfriend who had been hit also and wasn't moving.

Things were getting way out of hand too fast. The empty MAC10 in his hand with the bolt thrown open, smoke drifting out of it, was useless. Touw rolled twice to his right up against the wall, drawing his Beretta from his back. Roddy wasn't dead. Touw could see him breathing. He aimed precisely this time and pumped him with two more rounds. The body jerked and jolted as it was penetrated by the lead.

The Saturn engine bogged and then

stalled against the Bronco. Water from the crushed radiator sprayed into the air like a decorative fountain. Elena ran from the car out the exit of the garage.

Touw popped up athletically from his prone position, retrieving his MAC10 with his left hand. He pointed his Beretta in a circular motion looking for anybody hostile. This was the ugliest and most grotesque scene he'd ever experienced in his criminal career.

The driver's door on the Saturn opened as a staggering bloody mess stepped out. He squinted, not wanting to look, but having to. Nova looked like a burn victim except red instead of charred black. Her features were totally indiscernible. Flaps of skin from her cheeks hung down off her face with her teeth exposed, nothing covering them. An Ear was gone on one side, the mint green sweats now completely covered in blood.

She staggered around for a minute trying to find Touw, her arms flailing in the air. Touw stepped closer but kept arms' length away from her. Nova attempted to talk but couldn't as the blood sprayed from her exposed jugular vein each time her heart pumped. Desperately she reached for someone to hold her. Console her.

Touw couldn't handle it anymore. He took his 9mm and shot Nova in the head. Pow! The one shot echoed down the caverns of the parking lot.

"I'm doing you a favor, Nova."

For the first time ever Touw had the shakes. He was a mess. He felt sick to his stomach. No time for contemplation though. He re-holstered his Beretta and reseated a new clip into the MAC10. Curious onlookers were appearing and peaking around corners looking at the aftermath. So they want to test their bravery, get a quick thrill, Touw angrily summized. He was going to fix that real quick. A lot of confusion was what was needed for an escape. He took the MAC10 and unloaded another clip of thirty rounds in a hollow circle around his head. Deafening sound and sparks of bullets going off everywhere cleared the space of people instantly.

******

From above the Japantown parking lot complex it looked like somebody had let loose a pack of snakes in the building. People were pouring out of all the exits like water running down the street and diving into other doors blocks away. Gena looked on humorously as Steve studied the situation with care. He positioned the helicopter in a hover above the only exit for the Miokai garage. It was seemingly impossible to distinguish who and what was going on below other than bedlam. Suddenly the cell phone rang as he reached over to Gena, and she handed it to him.

Steve pressed talk, "Yeah!"

Touw's voice was barely discernible as it was obvious he was running at a full sprint trying to speak into it. "Blond girl, white, ran out the front entrance. She should be running," he gasped for his own breath. Shopping bag... Knife.. Down Geary toward the ocean! West!"

Daringly Steve dropped the helicopter down low, close enough to the ground to give himself away. He hovered forward down Geary one block, the power lines dangerously close to his rotors.

"Dirty blond, lean build," Touw screamed out.

"Got her," Steve announced. She gave herself away stopping to throw the shopping bag into a dumpster. No blond woman would ever throw something she just bought into a dumpster. Then in more of a panic she ran into oncoming traffic causing cars to swerve by the Arizona Room Jazz Club before cutting through the high-rise apartments by the Webster Safeway.

Steve climbed sharply, manhandling the 'copter to clear the building. He hoped to avoid vibrating the windows out of it. Steve and Gena watched the woman assassin slow to a walk composing her actions. She was clear from the immediate vicinity of the incident. Daringly she walked right along the outside of the police station on Fillmore and up Golden Gate to hail a cab. The police cars emptied out of the parking lot heading to seal off the embattled area. The woman even turned around to watch them daringly race up the one way street against traffic for the half a block on Turk before turning onto Fillmore. She was a pro all right. If she wasn't, she should be.

Steve was actually rooting for her. It did him no good if she got caught. His trail to Shoeghit would grow cold.

"Gena, hit redial and hand me the phone." She did and held it to his ear.

"Touw," Steve screamed into the phone. "You still there?"

"I'm in the car on the move!" His breathing was still labored trying to regain his breath.

"You going to make it?"

"I'll keep you advised."

"If you pick up a tail, remember back to when we discussed a parking garage where I could set down and pick you up?"

"Got it, it looks OK at the moment. Clearing as much space as I can. Traffic's bad. Gotta go." The phone clicked, dead. Steve nodded his head to Gena so she set the phone back in her lap.

"Gena, keep an eye on her while I circle around, we're getting a little too obvious." Steve pulled off and proceeded into a long arcing circle like a news copter would while filming a story.

"The bitch managed to hail a cab."

"Keep an eagle eye on it." The helo kept climbing to the very bottom of the cloud cover, turning around and picking up speed. Fortunately it was an small cab company. She had hailed a red station wagon from one of the struggling outfits. It stood out well from the air. Well enough for them to back way off to sit and watch. After only ten minutes the cab stopped at a house at the bottom of Twin Peaks. Elena the assassin got out and entered. No one left the residence after they had survailed it for fifteen minutes. She had given up the safe house.

Steve was charged up, "Now we're getting somewhere baby, dial Touw again." The phone connected.

"We're in business my friend. You OK?"

"Yes." Touw replied, more controlled, now.

"Our target has been identified. It's payback time."

"Good. Promise me you'll let me kill the bitch personally."

"I'll do my best, we don't have a lot of time. We need to move on it, and move on it now. Lose the car, but make sure we can get to it later. Get to escape area C. We'll need transportation, arrange it. I'll meet you there in twenty minutes. Bring all the gear."

"I understand, proceeding as we speak. Ah, Steve, one thing. Nova's gone. You realize that I guess."

"I had anticipated that might happen. It's just us now, Touw. We're the team."

"I'm a little shook up."

Steve acted surprised, "Really? You? That's a first."

"It was the way she died I guess."

"You'll have to fill me in later. Can you still work?"

"As long as we're heading in the direction of Shoeghit and his butchers, I'm not running from them ever. I refuse. I blame them for screwing up our lives, and I don't care what the circumstances are. No running. If you run, you run alone. Revenge is mine."

"No, we're not running. I think you'll like what I have in mind. Let me just say that it will be the biggest score in our history. Revenge is ours!"

Touw didn't answer Steve, he just hung up. A score wasn't on his mind. That's one of the reasons Steve was so fond of him. Money wasn't everything to him. Personal pride and honor drove Touw's heart.

"What are we doing?" Gena inquired.

"We're flying straight to San Francisco International Airport and landing. I'll rent tarmac space and have them fuel up the helo while we head back into the city. We'll duck into the terminal and meet Touw who should be arriving by cab. Whoever gets to the rentals first will get a car, and then we'll all come back into the city."

******

The Listener Thieves blasted out of SFO on a mission in a white Lincoln town-car. They briefly reveled in being united again, before returning to an all-business demeanor.

The sun had ducked behind the ocean, setting a half hour ago as darkness was drawing down more and more, covering the city. The nightly rains followed, sprinkling on the window of the car as they drove in.

Upon arriving at the scene of their target house, the team decided to case the building and the neighborhood hastily. They drove down Douglas Street where the target house was located. The street was a block long winding around the steep mountain of Twin Peaks. It ended in a cul-de-sac, so circling was out of the question.

The house looked small from the front as many of the SF houses did. It stood one floor, door centered in the middle with windows on either side of it. Upon making a U-turn and driving back to the street downhill from it, you could see that the residence extended back forty feet and down the hill two levels. A balcony off the back end of the entrance level had large windows. "That's the living room," Steve announced as he pulled over and parked on Eureka, the street below it. The lower floor had a deck leading to a steeply descending yard, and to one of the bedrooms. Lights were on in the back, but it was dark in the front.

"If a watch is posted it would be in the dark. You can peer out from behind the curtains with anonymity."

"I agree," Touw added.

On the way in Steve had hooked up a scanner out of the cigarette lighter port in the car. Now that they were stopped they focused a directional antenna at the house.

"Quiet in there. Nothing's going out over the air."

A man appeared in one of the lit windows at the rear of the house. He was big in stature and looked pissed off even from a distance.

"I'm thinking rear entrance, even though it's lit. What do you think, Touw?"

"I agree. Rear. The front's probably a fortress. We should angle in though, not directly through the yard. Barring dogs in one of the adjacent yards, we should enter from one of the back yards here on Eureka and climb into the adjacent yard to the target. Navigate up the hill quietly, and climb in off the neighbor's porch. Hopefully they won't be home. Jimmy the back screen-door and then when we're in—it's irrelevant after that. Showdown."

"Sounds like the plan, I'll make you a pact: you get the girl, I get Shoeghit. If possible."

"That's a deal."

"Enough talk," Steve announced reaching under the dash for the trunk button. "Let's get this done."

The two climbed out of the car, "Gena, you stay here," Steve commanded.

"No problem." Gena showed no desire for getting involved.

The two men dug through the trunk full of assorted weapons, tools, and electronic devices loaded earlier.

"No MAC10 this time Touw, I thought I would answer your question before you asked it. I know that's your favorite. We need to have some tact in doing this if we can. I want Shoeghit's cache. He's got to have every valuable thing he owns up there. We'll need some time to search. Use the silenced HK5's. Do this on the prowl."

Touw frowned in dislike. "I'm not a fan of bringing the muzzle velocity down below supersonic. It's like fighting with a BB gun. You can't shoot through anything."

"I know you too well, Touw. If I give you the MAC10 you'll aerate the whole block. The words "three round burst" are not in your vocabulary." Steve pulled the HK5 out and shoved it into Touw's hands. He also gave him a set of light intensifying goggles.

Touw ran the weapons functions expediently making sure everything was in working order, then gave Steve a nod, he was ready.

After putting on the goggles the two walked silently across the semi-dark Eureka Street and in between the houses below their target. The overcast skies that drizzled sporadic rain completely blocked out the moonlight. This made it mostly dark even with the light intensifiers. Trees cast distorted shadows as they waved eerily in the wind.

A red fence sectioned off the back yards. Steve made a little knocking noise on it with the tip of his silencer to stir any dogs that might be sleeping.

No response.

He reached over and opened the gate and walked into the back yard.

Frustrated, not being able to see well enough to his liking, Touw pulled his goggles down around his neck. He grabbed the back of Steve's shirt and let him tow him along while he searched his senses for unusual feelings. The light rain dripped down the mens' stern, killing faces as they made the rear fence dividing the two yards.

Steve wiped the rain off his optics as he peered up into the back of the target house from over the fence. Touw wasn't looking. He was transfixed by the moving and swaying shadows like a little kid scared of the dark. It was a grotesquely rotten, eerie night out. The demons were all about them. Touw could feel it.

"Come on! Snap out of it. Look at where the hell you're going," Steve said quietly but urgently, looking back. The spikes of tiny rain-drops unsympathetically stabbed their exposed faces. "Approach from the adjacent yard, climb the fence now. Do it!" Steve said angrily.

Touw moved, topping the fence like it wasn't there, Steve hurried to keep up. Steve had seen this in Touw before. He was a very spiritual, sensitive person. Certain events tended to wig him out. He was scared of no man, but fanatically frightened of things that he couldn't touch, like shadows, ghostly sounds, the wind.

Steve caught up to him as he was rapidly leaving him behind. He grabbed a hand full of his wet shirt in the spot between his shoulder blades. They were at the corner of the house now and it was too late to say anything. They climbed silently up onto the porch of the house next door to the target. Touw's unwavering stare was fixed on the target as he pressed on, stepping over the low fence and onto the lit back porch of the target house.

Steve happened to glance into the window of the neighbors' house they were using for a spring board, assuming it was empty. Chills ran down his spine to see a little kid in his room staring out from under the covers of his bed. Only his eyes were visible. Realizing he must look like the bogey man with all his gear on, Steve held his arms up high in the air in a haunting manner and extending his cold fingers out like claws. He squashed his face against the window distorting it into flat shapes, scaring the crap out of the boy who disappeared under the security of his blanket. Steve bolted away over the fence into the next yard, becoming only a bad dream in the kid's memory.

The bottom section of the house was all lit. Two rooms shared the wall along with a back sliding door to the porch area. Touw crawled below window level and was already jimmying the latch to the screen with his pocket knife.

Steve incited himself. "Here we go!"

There was always no waiting around when Touw got focused. The screen broke open and the two bolted in as if suction had taken control of their bodies. Their silenced gun barrels hunted for targets, leading every step they took. They were in a torn-apart bedroom, completely ransacked. Closet opened, clothes on the floor, hangers thrown everywhere. TV knocked off the dresser onto the floor, the screen cracked.

The sound of a loud argument was reverberating from the forward part of the bottom half of the house just two walls' distance from where they were. They were arguing so loudly they couldn't have heard the two enter. Steve and Touw framed the door to the room standing off to the sides quietly listening.

"Fuck you, you bitch, Shoeghit said that you were supposed to share part of that money with me!"

"No he didn't. He'll take care of you later. It's mine."

"So, you're telling me I didn't hear what I heard with my own two ears."

"I don't know what you think you heard, or what you think you're going to pull on me, but that's my money and it goes to me. I charge one hundred thousand a hit, and that's a hundred grand."

The man's voice strained to its highest level of anger without screaming. "You calling me a liar!?"

"Call it what you want, that money goes with me."

The argument continued just barely in control, on the verge of breaking into a fight. Steve forced out a devilish smile to Touw and nodded. Steve rounded the corner of the door and stepped guardedly up the hall to the door to the back room with the arguing couple. He raised his hand at Touw, pointing up the stairs to the top floor, the level even with the street.

Steve turned the corner of the doorway and stepped into the room aiming down on the two. The conversation stopped abruptly as they looked at him in shock. Their expressions said what their mouths didn't: "Where did you come from?"

"Drop the guns now!" Steve commanded. The two had been having an argument over money with pistols in their hands. Steve cursed his luck. If he had only waited a little bit, they would have solved the situation.

"DROP THEM!"

Steve's "drop them," statement echoed up the stairs as Touw was running up them in a mercenary mode. Any hope of surprise had been compromised by the noise. The guard at the door would surely have been alerted. At the top of the steps he crouched down knowing it was coming. BOOM! A shot rang out from the front door going through the wall at the spot the guard had guessed Touw would be standing.

Touw acted out the scene. He banged his elbow on the wall as if he had fallen, and cried out a simulated painful gasp. Touw looked back through the hole in the wall the shotgun blast had made, eying the approaching assailant. Touw thrust the barrel of the HK5 up to it. The silenced noise of the bullets spraying out the business end of the gun and the real thump of a body falling down after being punctured numerous times fueled Touw's confidence. He rolled out into the hall shooting the man laying up against the wall two more times to make sure he was dead.

Touw regained his feet and started meticulously checking the rooms for any more guards.

Back downstairs two guns bounced off the floor as they were dropped.

"Hands up!" Steve winced as his captives jumped slightly from the shots ringing out upstairs. The following muffled burst and thump of a body falling comforted his anxieties.

"First," Steve directed to the man, "Who are you?"

The man didn't respond, staring back defiantly.

Steve dropped the barrel of his gun to his knee and shot, POP! The man's leg cracked open in a backwards motion partially coming apart at the knee. The man fell over, while Steve instantly retrained his gun on Elena. "Who is he?"

"One of Shoeghit men," Elena answered.

"Is Shoeghit here?"

"No..." Elena began to answer casually.

The man on the floor, said something to her in Hebrew.

Steve turned the gun on him and shot him again in the stomach once. "You were saying?"

This time she was a little unnerved. "He's on his way to his boat in Tiburon."

"Is that his hideout?"

"No." She looked at Steve like he's not too quick. "He's sailing to Mexico tonight, and then flying to Israel when he gets some new papers. He's leaving all of us behind to suffer the consequences of his actions. I don't care. I just want my money. Can I go?"

"What's the name of the boat?"

"Path to Bliss." It's a yacht actually."

Footsteps could be heard coming down the stairs, as Steve quickly called out while backing up to a wall, "Touw is that you?"

"Yes," he said calmly as he walked into the room. "Ah...there she is," Touw said. Pupupupupop. Touw mowed Elena down viciously.

"Ah SHIT!," Steve yelled out scoldingly, the blood splattering all over him. "Not yet damn it!"

"You said I could kill her."

"Yes, but... Oh well. Never mind," Steve shot the wounded man in the head uncaringly and walked to the bed. He grabbed the gym bag full of money. "Let's go. We've got a lot more work to get done.

9

Monday morning 10:30AM. Touw circled the block around the Frank Ross campaign headquarters before parking. He was a little freaked out at the idea of walking into a building with over ten police officers and a number of security personnel stationed around it. Squad cars and news vans lined the perimeter of the building like a picture frame. Parking the car well away from the entrance Touw approached slowly, adjusting the tie on his fifteen hundred dollar suit as he walked.

He focused his center on staying calm. Normally a regular citizen would have a nervous persona going to see a candidate, he reminded himself. The tension should be magnified due to current events, so he shouldn't look suspicious. "Just be you," Touw coaxed himself. "Well...be a nicer you." At the entrance to the offices, news team six's reporter Jimmy Lanier was speaking into his camera live. Touw stopped to hear what he had to say.

"Today just outside the Frank Ross headquarters the mood is quiet. The offices stand virtually empty of people. Stark contrast to an area once brimming-full of campaign volunteers and enthusiastic workers. His supporters have dwindled to nothing, replaced by heavily armed police officers. As you look behind me at the deserted tables you must remember just yesterday hundreds of democracy-loving Americans were working out their electoral process. Now in disbelief the disheartened volunteers stay home. No one but the entourage of police attempting to stop this rapidly out-of-control violence. Yes, volunteers replaced by swat teams: how low have we stooped in this country? The San Francisco political scene looks more like a South American fascist election. Instead of men walking around with AK-47s we have police with M16s."

Jimmy pointed to the roof of a hotel across the street with a police sniper peering over it. His rifle barrel hung out over the ledge ready to shoot instantly.

"For the first time ever Channel Six news will not be endorsing a candidate in a mayoral election. It is the opinion of Channel Six that due to the events of the last three days we wish to keep the incumbent administration in office to create stability in the city."

Touw listened, his hands cupped behind his back in a non-threatening manner. It was the first time he had ever seen an un-endorsement. He giggled, slightly amused.

"As a direct result of the violence that Frank

Ross has been accused of being tied to, the campaign has fallen considerably in the polls. At the end of the week, Friday, the Ross campaign was dead even with Larry Bennard. Now the candidate is only at twenty percent voter approval rating in the city. Richard Morris, replacing the deceased mayor, is running away with the polls at sixty-five percent approval, leaving only fifteen percent undecided. The calm over the city seems to be holding this morning. We will be following these events as they unfold throughout the day. Jimmy Lanier, Channel Six news."

The camera on the tripod's red light turned off as the camera man hurriedly disassembled the equipment and loaded the van. Jimmy clicking off the switch on his microphone looked at Touw, his only audience, and winked. He stepped past Touw heading for the van giving him a squeeze on the shoulder. "What do you think?" he asked.

"I try not to." Touw ignored the chumminess and walked off. As he entered the campaign office, he was immediately met at the door by two police officers. They motioned with outstretched arms to stop. "Sir, please hold your hands out like this. We must pat you down for security reasons."

Touw complied smiling and nodding.

The two officers checked him very aggressively not allowing for any timidness in the personal areas. "Your business sir?"

"Ahh yes, my name is David Tran. I had promised to stop and see Frank this week."

"Yes sir. Would you please have a seat while we confirm?"

"Certainly." Touw sat on the same sofa he had to sit on the last time he had been here.

The receptionist called upstairs, talking for a moment and then nodded to the cops. An officer in a gray suit from behind the two at the door came up and motioned to Touw to follow him. Diligently the officer tagged right beside Touw all the way up the stairs and to the door of Frank Ross's office.

The upstairs scene at the office looked pathetic at best. Empty seats and desks piled deep with papers. Only two employees were left to endure the work load. Both had phones to their ears. Their heads were down, buried in their computer.

Frank Ross, the stoic authoritarian who would normally sit at his desk and wait for someone to come in, was at his door smiling happily at Touw.

"Hello Mr. Tran. I see this insanity didn't scare you. Come in, come in." Frank waved to the cop, "It's OK."

Touw walked into Frank Ross's office shutting

the door behind him, himself. Frank patted Touw on the shoulder as he walked by. "It's good to see you my friend."

The two men sat down. The tone had been hurried the last time they had met, now it was if they had nothing in the world pending for them.

"These events that have transpired are really absurd. This whole Shoeghit thing's out of control. I don't know how they keep linking him to me. It was their plan all along. The good news is, David, we are going to be cleared from being implicated in this soon. The police have a couple of hot leads they're tracing and when they get Shoeghit, they will clear me of all wrong-doing. Then with Larry out of the picture, I'm a shoe-in to win the election." Frank reclined back in his chair acting relaxed.

The day outside was warm, the sun had burned off all the clouds from the night's rains. Frank had all his shades pulled down on the windows, denying himself the beautiful sunlight and denying the media the chance to photograph the empty campaign headquarters. The inactivity was evidence of his ruined career.

"So, Mr Tran, I'm very pleased that you decided to come down after all these problems. Believe me, the people that stick with me through all this are going to be rewarded. We're badly in need of money right now. Can you help?"

"I figured that," Touw responded.

"Trust me though, David. Everything's going to be fine. The wheels of justice are grinding away. This will all be settled shortly. I'll be handling all the financial situations myself, if you know what I mean." Frank smiled humorously. "In fact, I've already tasked your money for a commercial on Wednesday. It explains what has happened. The frame-job those Jews did on me. Those criminals have tried to wipe me out. And since they didn't get their way they tried to destroy the whole city. Shoeghit's going to get the chair for this. People who know me realize that I would be smarter than to let a criminal control me. The accusations are false.

Touw smiled and then broke out in laughter. He laughed out loud uncontrollably for a moment and then regained his composure.

Frank Ross was a little taken back by the humorous eruption. He didn't find it that humorous, only smiling inquisitively back at Touw.

Now Touw sat back confidently in his chair staring knowingly at Frank Ross. "I'm going to stop you before you make any more of an ass out of yourself than you've already done."

The expression on Frank Ross's face grew cool, replaced by a rigid stare. His talented manipulative knifing eyes would have made a normal person squirm in their seat. He sat listening.

"I didn't bring any green stuff for you to piss away on this washed-up campaign. The only thing you would have done with it is stick it in your fat, empty pocket. You and I know you're fucking out of this city the minute this show's over."

Frank started to say something, but Touw held up his hand and stopped him.

"You just hold on there, Mr. Politician. I got something you're going to want to look at before you open your fat mouth." Touw reached into his jacket pocket and produced some papers, throwing them on the desk.

Picking up the copies and recognizing them instantly Frank looked back at Touw as if now he knew the answer to a problem that had daunted him. He leaned forward, putting his elbows on his desk, not saying a word.

"I'm not good with codes, but my boss is. He'll fiddle for months trying to solve a mystery. I bet over time we could figure out what all that's about. I'm not good with addresses either, but if I was a betting man, I would wager that most of those addresses go to Shoeghit, or shall we say Shoeghit's concerned parties. We also have a copy of the infamous video tape of your political consultant Jack Swanson getting his guts spilled by your employee Ivan. It happened in some hard-to-explain circumstances. Would you like me to mail a copy of that to you? And maybe to the news as well?"

Frank didn't respond. He just stared.

"Do I have your attention?"

"You got balls coming down here. I could have you arrested right now."

"For what? Bringing you a bunch of documents that don't exist? Photocopies even? We got you, Ross. You're going to do exactly as we say," Touw asserted firmly.

"Who's we? To whom am I talking? Are you representing somebody?"

"Let's just say we're the new power brokers in this city. You want to climb, you placate us. Or we'll crush you."

"I don't like this," Frank said defiantly. He picked up a pencil and started bouncing the eraser on the desk nervously.

"Why?" Touw asked. "You dealt with that dick-head Shoeghit."

"I did not!"

"Oh yes you did. He was pulling your strings. Your, I guess you could call it, puppet-master." Touw broke a little evil grin at the insult.

Frank Ross held his tongue, preferring to stare angrily.

"Come on, Frank. You know how to play ball. Hey, you remember Shoeghit's friend, the older gal?" Touw said whimsically. "Oh, what was her name...my boss told me...ahh...Elena. Yeah, that's it. You remember her?"

"No, I don't."

"Oh. Well that's a good thing because she's dead. Got her brains blown out."

"It means nothing."

"Ah, yes, of course. Funny, I bet I could get twenty or thirty of your volunteers to remember her coming up to your office. And now she's dead. Well, what could that infer?

"What do you what from me David?" Frank said, giving in.

"Just two little things."

"Go ahead. I'm listening."

"First you're going to make a call to one of your supporters and leave a message. One we tell you to leave."

"Who?"

"The Caulfield's. Secondly, you withdraw from the race tonight at eight o'clock on television."

Frank waited before responding, fuming angrily at his desk, "And the alternative?"

"We implicate you in the murder of Mayor Bennard and make it stick. The cops will believe anything at this point. You're a marked man.

You ever been in jail before?"

"So that's the way it is."

"Yes. Don't be disheartened though. You may be mayor next time if we decide. We can't salvage your campaign now, though. It's too late. You step down, cooperate. We'll take good care of you."

******

Gena noticed Steve was in a more festive mood as the crew settled in to their new operating base. He clearly felt in control of the situation, shifting it to his advantage. Outside the RV Touw and Steve clanged and clattered adjusting the two stroke motor that powered the generator. The Winnebago was well weathered: still nice but more than worn-in. The rental's small motor finally chugged to life and the inside lights brightened correspondingly. As it settled into a steady hum, Steve replaced the cover to the motor, screwing it down tight.

The two walked back around to the door and reentered the motor home, slamming the door shut.

"Do you think we got a big enough house?" Touw asked sarcastically. The two men shrugged off the cold breeze whipping over the mountain top.

"One mobile headquarters. *Ta Daa.*" Steve put his hand out in a presentational manner. He reached down turning on the electric heater to warm everything up. "So what's for dinner Gena?"

Contentedly she broke open the refrigerator that had been sealed shut for traveling and checked the stores of food they had picked up on the way out to the Oakland Airport a day ago. "On the menu we have Salisbury steak TV dinner or turkey TV dinner. Also, we have baloney sandwiches. For your beverage," she held out a large container, "You have your choice of juice, juice with vodka, vodka, or water."

Touw smiled, giggling at her candor, "I'll take turkey, and juice."

"I'm feeling like Salisbury steak and water," Steve added.

A overflow of electronics equipment crammed the top of the dining table in the large motor home. A beamed-style mood light shone down on it from the overhead shelves. Three cell phones, a lap top computer, with Internet connection. Two sets of scanners, stacked three deep in front of the window, plus a TV. Damage proof suitcases stacked behind the driver's seat with bugs, lock picking tools, safe cracking drills—everything a thief could want.

Gena uncovered the cellophane from the carton of one of the dinners and stuck it in the microwave.

"Hey aren't you supposed to leave that on?" Touw inquired, "That's what it says on the carton."

"No, it's OK to take it off."

"Are you sure? I've been a bachelor for years, and I always just open a corner."

"Ah...come on Touw, live on the edge. Take a walk on the wild side and remove the cellophane." Gena keyed in the time and turned it on.

"Yeah, Touw, you wimp," Steve added whimsically. "OK. Let's review the precautions to keep Shoeghit from escaping the country and see if we missed anything. First, the Coast Guard has been alerted that the most wanted man in America will try to escape throughthe bay by boat. We tipped them that Shoeghit had access to a boat but it is located at an undetermined marina inside the bay so he must exit through the Golden Gate. That will thwart an early try at it, at least for a day. The Coasties' manpower will be exhausted soon trying to check all the boats leaving, but that will keep him put for a day or two."

Touw, listening still, got up and walked to the rear of the Winnebago, to the walled off part. It was a small bedroom. The bed, normally centered in the middle, was unbolted and pushed to the side. A huge set of binoculars peered out the window through the drawn shade off a tripod stand. Touw looked in them gazing at the Caulfield's house checking both the front and rear exits. "I'll take the first watch," he spoke loudly back to Steve, interjecting into his conversation. The rear bedroom and the bathroom were the only separated parts of the RV. Touw adjusted the chair as he settled in for his watch. "Sorry, I didn't mean to interrupt. Did you call the police about all the hideouts?"

"Yes," Steve said, making some notes on a piece of paper. "Tipped the PD to all Shoeghit's safe houses. Except for the Caulfield's," he mumbled to himself. "I bet old Shoeghit's feeling a little stranded about right now. They're probably redoing all his escape plans as we speak."

Touw's voice traveled out from the darkened back bedroom area. "I wish you would let me climb down that hill and set up my rifle. I've been itching to use it. One shot, one kill. Bam right across the valley through the window. Spray his brains all over the Caulfield's dinner table."

"I know, Touw. Think of the reward though, the back end. There has got to be two or three million in cash traveling with him. Secret money no one will miss. No one to report it stolen after we take it. Our biggest heist ever. The perfect crime. And with the bonus of not having any remorse for the victim."

Steve fiddled with the scanners as he talked, programming them to certain frequencies. The warmth from the heater started to relax the crew more. There was no longer a briskness to the air inside the RV. The cold wind outside slightly rocked the big squared vehicle as it blew hard. The rains had desisted, leaving a clear night.

While watching the target mansion loosely, Touw spread the cache of weapons out on the bed. He ran patches down the barrels and Q-tipped the firing mechanisms clean in his lap. It was second nature. The two silenced Heckler and Koch MP5's lay above the MAC10 he used in the garage incident. The sniping rifle leaning against the bed post was of Russian origin. He had picked it up at a surplus gun show in Phoenix. It was wrapped in a formed cloth case to protect the polished wood. Two glock 9mm's were also at the bottom of the bed. That was all the artillery they had except for the two Berettas they both carried all the time. Such a small amount for a operation that was on its way to taking control of the city. It just proved cunning always outwitted brawn.

Steve had rigged up a couple of small gunpowder charges. They were small angled metal plates with cloth and duct tape around them, plus a fuse. These homemade shaped charges could be placed on a door lock, or a hinge to blast them open quickly. Carefully he placed them in a small back pack so they could be grabbed at an instant. Touw reveled in his weaponry. He excitedly anticipated using them.

Gena lovingly brought Touw his food to nourish his hunger. The turkey TV dinner, steaming hot on top of a towel, smelled good after not having eaten anything for a couple of days. She set it down beside him, laying out a plastic fork and spoon neatly along with a big plastic tumbler of juice.

"Thank you, Gena," Touw said warmly back to her in appreciation. He was flattered by her caring attention to detail.

"I'll be up front if you need me."

"Sure."

He sipped the juice holding his hand up to the heater vent in back. The warmth was finally making its way to the back of the RV.

Up front, Steve studied a map of the house's grounds he had drawn up. The Caulfields had crossed more than a few people's paths in their business dealings. A lot of powerful businessmen had vendettas to cash in against them. Their multi-million dollar house was a fortress. They weren't taking any chances.

Steve had bought himself some time. He had

to make sure Shoeghit would stay put 'til night fall this Monday. To do that, he had Touw make Frank Ross call Shoeghit's voice mail and the Caulfield's home telling them that if they could locate him, "Tell him not to leave yet." Ostensibly, the stall was so that he could clear Shoeghit and would exonerate him at an eight o'clock news conference. He stated that there was a secret video that the police had that showed the shooting in the mayor's office, clearing him of all wrong doing. It was from a hidden camera used only for extreme emergencies.

The real slap in the face Steve had arranged was that instead of exonerating Shoeghit, Frank Ross would withdraw from the race leaving Shoeghit as food for the political piranhas to eat. He'd stipulate being unfairly linked to the Shoeghit syndicate, so that he may run again next election for a city council spot. This put us into an even more powerful position by him denying the association and us having proof of events of it occurring.

While Shoeghit sat fuming at the double-cross, that's when we would move. He'd be saturated with anger, not able to think straight.

The hillside mansion was a nightmare to attack. It looked like a fortress from the old days of Germany, completely surrounded by a large wall. Hidden in a channel behind the dark brown trim were razor wire bundles around the entire perimeter. The large iron gate at the front was impenetrable and monitored by a guard. Every thirty feet on the wall was a camera with a light and a motion detector. The steep hill the house was on dropped into Richardson Bay making silent movement almost impossible.

Inside, Rottweilers roamed the entire grounds unrestricted. A guard in front had an armored console and a second guard was posted on the dock with a radio.

Steve pondered his regrets at not being a Navy Seal. He wished he could swim up from underneath the dock and enter in that manner. That just wasn't going to happen though. Taking this fortress was going to be the pinnacle of his career, or his demise. Either way he was set for the rest of his life. Rich or dead.

The Salisbury steak dinner smelled good to his very hungry body. Gena slid it onto the only open part of the table, then put her hands on Steve's shoulders massaging them. They watched an update on the small television mounted in the side of the kitchen cabinet space.

"Jimmy Lanier Channel 6 news. We want to call your attention to a special news conference scheduled by the candidate for mayor, Frank Ross, at 8:00 pm tonight, just an hour and an half from now. It hasn't been disclosed what the subject matter will be, but our sources inside the campaign say that Frank Ross will withdraw from the campaign."

"Fuck it all to hell!" Steve bellowed out. "Can't those fucking idiots keep anything a secret? They must of bugged his office. Did you hear that Touw?"

"Yes, relax Steve, it's OK. They haven't moved an inch. We'll take them no matter what."

"Is everything OK?" Gena asked.

"Yes, I suppose. I just wish the media wouldn't speculate. Shoeghit ain't going nowhere. At least 'til eight o'clock, after that he might run."

Gena ran her hand through his long curly hair. Her breasts rubbed up against the back of Steve's head. Steve smiled and turned around not saying a word. The Salisbury steak was left to grow cold as the two climbed up into the bedbunk above the driver's seats and drew the curtain shut.

In the rear Touw diligently observed the mansion below through the binoculars. He had to readjust the aim as the RV kept moving slightly. "Damn tremors."

******

8:00pm. Steve and Touw sat in the war car outside the Caulfields' estate just around the bend from the front gates. They left Gena behind up on the hill to watch the RV. The large old trees of the ritzy area swayed in the strong wind creating whistling noises. The two thieves sat listening intently to the live broadcast of Frank Ross withdrawing from campaign activities for this year. He followed their instructions to a tee this time, stating "he needed time to clear his name of all wrongdoing."

Suddenly a vehicle pulled up and stopped behind them. A spot light lit up the interior of the war car.

"Ah shit!" Steve said out loud. With a worried look, he turned Touw from the driver's seat. "This is trouble, big trouble."

The two men were sitting in the car with silenced HK5's in their laps. Still worse two pistols each and black jump suits on. In the back pack were explosives and every lock-picking aid under the sun. Just being where they were, with the weapons, without doing anything more, was ten years in prison. The car had approached with the lights off only illuminating them at the last second. With the strong wind blowing, they didn't even hear it.

Touw's hand cocked the HK5 then gripped down tightly on the handle. Steve looked over guardedly, then cocked his, seeing no way out. The spotlight was blinding and they couldn't see back without looking obvious. It was impossible to tell if there was one cop or two. Or still worse, a number of cars behind them backing the initial car up.

A figure approached hugging the blind spot of the car. Not sure of what to do Steve rolled the window down. The second the cop got within sight of looking in, he'd see the weaponry, There was no way to hide it.

Touw didn't wait. He lifted the HK5 up, setting the muzzle onto the back of Steve's seat and aimed through the back window. Pop, pop, pop, the silencer barely restrained the noise as the back door window shattered and the uniformed man fell to his back in the middle of the road. Steve burst out the door dropping to the cold ground looking for more targets. Touw crawled across and slipped out the same side. He crouched in a duck walk and went to the patrol car while Steve covered him from the prone position.

At the car Touw stood straight up and reached into the driver's side turning out the lights. He ran back to the war car and set his HK5 on the roof.

"It's one of those private patrols. Quick, let's get him back in his car and park it over under the trees there."

Steve sprung up grabbing the dead security guard under one arm while Touw latched onto his shirt and drug him back to the patrol car.

"You OK, Boss?"

"Yes," Steve answered, "I have no sympathy for people that protect the rich." They stuffed his body in the back after opening the door. "All these ultra rich fucks steal, evict, and rob people on a daily basis. This four-dollar-an-hour dick-head protects them from his own kind. He deserved what he got. We need to make our move now. He might have called in."

"He didn't call in."

"How do you know?"

"They would be calling for him by now. Check on him. He just got careless playing Johnny Law."

The two briskly walked back to the car after stashing the security car. "Let's do it," Steve said as they grabbed all their gear out.

The mansions in Tiburon-by-the-Bay were spread apart generally about three hundred yards, set on the steep side of the hills. They all had their own private docks with big yachts.

The two thieves disappeared into the brush and crawled up to fifty yards from the large brick wall on the side of the estate. They lay in the still muddy ground from all the rain. The freezing wind whirled between the trees giving a good noise cover to their movement.

Steve held up a piece of filtered glass to his

eyes, while Touw attached a scope to the top of his assault rifle by sticking it on at a ninety degree angle and then turning it 'til it snapped into place, straight forward.

"Lasers..." Steve said, "Across the top of the wall just above the razor wire."

"OK," Touw acknowledged taking aim. "Say when."

"When."

Pop! Touw squeezed off one round. The bullet smashed through the motion sensor on the bottom of the light. He looked through his scope again to be sure he had hit his mark.

"Good hit."

"OK," Steve raised up to his feet staying in a crouch, slowly approaching the wall at the side of the mansion. It was an intimidating obstacle. Steve felt like his ancestors must have in the days of beseiging castles in Europe. The overlapping cameras covered forty foot sections of the fortresses outside. Although they could see relatively well in the low light, the guards were used to an instant illumination from the motion lights to draw their attention to the video monitor. Black coveralls and black ski masks camouflaged them in the dark, making them invisible.

Steve knew they would be safe as they stood just outside the wall. He shouldered his HK5, then clasped his hands and gave Touw a knee up so he could grab the edge of the wall top.

Steadying himself, leaning against the wall with his feet on each of Steve's shoulders, Touw placed mirrors on tripods on the top of the wall. He carefully measured to see that they were at perfect ninety degree angles. Gently he slid them into the lasers' fields, one on each side making a gap three feet wide.

He then hoisted himself up standing on the piece of ledge just inside the razor wire. From his backpack he removed two large magnets and stuck them into the razor wire. The strands clumped to it, and he parted them as far as they could spread. He smiled, thinking to himself, "We're in." A cheep one-hook grapple was the next item pulled from his backpack. He wedged the hook in the drainage ravine at the top of the wall and lowered the knotted line down to Steve.

Like a cat Steve ascended to the top of the wall. Touw stood like a conqueror straight up peering down on the inside of the compound. At the top Steve grabbed the line reeling it up, and lowered it down the other side of the wall.

Touw was removing the scope from the HK5 so it wouldn't be in the way of his killing aim.

Steve blew the dog whistle they had picked up at the pet store. Like magic the three Rottweilers turned the corner of the back of the house, alerted by the high decibel tone only a dog could hear. They sniffed and checked the area, one noticing the rope dangling down from the wall as a new smell. Above on the wall the two thieves unsympathetically picked them off with their silenced guns. Two fell instantly as if their legs had been cut out from under them. The last one looked at his friends, not understanding what had happened when his end was given him from above. The freezing strong wind, gusting across the valley, was a real blessing to the mission of this night.

The two thieves lowered into the compound silently. The inside yard to the mansion was beautiful: lush green grass framed tastefully by sculpted bushes. Behind the bushes mood lighting cast elegant shadows. The different entrances to the house had large columns on either side of the doors. All the tops to the windows were rounded with Art Deco swirls up and down them.

It was eerily silent except for the wind blowing. Almost as if they knew it was coming. Rich people were always a spooky lot when you entered their personal lives.

Steve approached the side door with the silenced muzzle of the HK5 leading and pointing everywhere he stepped. He tried the handle while Touw peered into the window next to it looking for trouble inside. The solid oak door was bolted shut. No way they were going to make an entrance here without a lengthy and dangerous lock-picking session. He motioned to Touw to fall in behind him without making a noise as he headed for the rear of the house.

Not a noise from inside. No television, music, conversation, nothing. Warily they slowly descended a set of eight steps down on the side of the house following the contour to the lowest level of the three. They came into view of the guard on the dock who wasn't looking their way at the time. He was content with trying to stay warm.

A patio encircled the lower level of the mansion in a U-shape. Expensive outdoor furniture with a redwood hot tub in the corner. From the porch surrounding the lower level the hill dropped almost straight off. A long wooden stairway descended steeply down to the private dock where the two different boats were moored. One was a cigarette style speed boat and the other a double-masted sail boat at least forty four feet.

The porch creaked slightly at the weight of the two men on it. Steve eased back on his step. He rounded the corner aiming into the big glass window with a centered sliding door. Inside drapes were pulled shut the entire length.

Whaaa! The fog horn under the Golden Gate Bridge went off, making both the thieves jump. They squatted down hiding out of sight of the guard on the pier.

Steve pulled on the sliding door. It opened.

He pulled it back only enough to squeeze through to the inside. They slid through shutting it again. In the three foot gap between the curtain and the large windows they sat and listened. A shadow of a human figure emerged into the room and walked by making no noise, then exited to the back.

Bravely Steve pulled the curtain apart and entered the room. The house was the picture of the opulent life style. Light brown painted walls with built-in book shelves, sporting a huge library. Piano, expensive vases with fresh cut flowers in them. Fine art, framed and lit exquisitely. It was almost too pretty to live in.

Suddenly, from the back room, one of the Caulfields stumbled out with a martini in her hand, an older lady with silvery brown hair. Her skin stretched tight from a number of face-lifts, she looked up blurry-eyed at the two men adorned in black almost as if she were hallucinating. Touw lunged forward covering the distance with three huge steps, pulling his leg back into a side kick and thrusting it up into her jaw karate style. The small woman's head popped back making a snapping sound as her whole body hit the floor solidly. The martini glass literally stayed frozen in the air after her hand fell away from it and Touw grabbed it before it fell. Steve leaned in behind him removing the glass from Touw's hand and taking a sip from it.

"Nice touch," he whispered to Touw. "Shitty Martini though."

A sinister laugh came from the back room of the bottom floor of the mansion. A man laughing hard and rudely. Touw and Steve took cover up against the wall.

"Ha, ha, ha, you dumb broad. Drinky drink fall over. Hehehe." A man stumbled out from the back hall looking down at the woman out on the floor. "You dumb bitch. How many times are you going to fucking pass out?" He swayed as he lectured the body on the floor, pointing and shaking his finger at her. So drunk, he was oblivious to Steve stepping up from behind him.

"Dumb bitch that's all you are. You've always been a dumb bitch. I don't know why I keep you around. I'll show you...I'm leaving your drunken ass on the floor tonight. You're sleeping right there. No blanket, nothing." As he lectured, blood trickled out from her ear onto the hardwood floor. "Oh now, look what you've done. Cut yourself. Well bleed to death bitch. I need a new wife. Hey, I'll even get out of alimony if you die! Die Bitch, die!" The man laughed.

Steve had had enough of the bantering idiot. He grabbed him like a vice around the neck in a choke hold, cutting off his air. The man's arms flailed wildly, completely surprised at the attack. Touw walked around and jabbed the guy firmly in the sternum, causing the man to fall to his knees. Within seconds, the man was dead. He fell in a heap over the body of his wife. Steve could still hear the man's evil laugh in his head. He wouldn't be losing any sleep over that death tonight.

Painstakingly the two thieves worked the rooms of the bottom floor, many guest bedrooms off the living space, all empty. They paused for a moment before making for the second floor, listening upstairs for foot traffic. Creaks in the floor, talking nothing. These people are like ghosts, he speculated. Steve nodded and pointed to the stairs.

Touw began the ascent to the second floor. He panned right and left with his HK5 working the entire space in front of him. At the top he leaned up to look in when a hand with a taser reached through the banister and jammed it into Touw's neck. The voltage tensed his body contorting it. Touw struggled futilely trying to release himself from the prods but couldn't, falling limp.

Steve capped off three rounds from his silenced HK5 into the floor above him, but they didn't have the velocity to penetrate.

The hand pulled the taser away, disappearing.

Steve attempted to stop Touw from falling backwards down the stairs, grabbing for his coveralls but had to let Touw tumble down beside him after spotting a shadow moving above.

BADA, BADA, DAT. Steve sprayed the whole entrance to the second floor emptying his clip. Left hand jammed the clip release and it fell out bouncing down the stairs right behind Touw. Steve seated another clip lightning fast, his life depending on it.

Haaa! He screamed out charging forward up the stairs. At the top he reached up with just his gun and shot one shot each direction then quickly peeked through the banister. It was a large double sized hall once tastefully decorated, now destroyed.

His eyes adjusted to the light in the hall as he ascended the final steps, looking for a target to kill. Hugging the left side of the wall he guardedly walked up to the first door. A noise from behind startled him. He wrenched around starting to pull the trigger as a huge muscular guard in a black shirt tackled him jamming his shoulder into his chest like a linebacker. Steve

tried to divert the energy but was toppled
backwards, slamming to the floor. Shoeghit ran
out from behind another door and latched on to
Steve's HK5 trying to pull it from him.

"Let go of the gun, Steve," Shoeghit screamed
out, as his guard put a knee in Steve's chest to
hold him down, the guard assisting pulling on the
HK5. Steve pinned down, let go of the HK5 as
the two pulling on it repelled back from the
removal of resistance. Too fast to counter,
Steve's nimble safe cracking hands drew his
Beretta and fired three rounds into the chest of
the guard. Shoeghit ran for the stairs. Steve shot
four rounds hitting him in the hand as he turned
and disappeared up the stairs to the top level.

Pissed off at missing, Steve kicked the guard
the rest of the way off him and shot the last two
rounds out of his Berretta into his head.

He picked up his HK5, but Shoeghit had
jammed it wedging the hammer back. No time to
fuck with it. He took his only other berretta clip
and seated it, locked and loaded. A bit staggered,
Steve went for the stairs. He quieted himself,
trying to compose his rapid breathing. Upstairs
he could hear Shoeghit breaking all the lights
out.

Diligently one step at a time Steve slowly
ascended the stairs. It was very dark. Only the
light from below and some shadows cast through

the windows illuminated the top floor. He saw a figure at the end of the hall in the large door way. Bam! Steve fired.

He listened as he crouched down behind an old couch.

"Not very fair to shoot at an unarmed opponent," a voice erupted from the dark.

"Since when have you ever been fair?" Steve replied. His eyes hunted wildly for the source of the voice.

Suddenly Shoeghit stepped out from a door one closer than the last. Bam, Steve fired but he didn't fall. Bam, bam, he fired two more as the coat fell off the broom handle. "God," Steve scolded himself, "How could you fall for that?"

Shoeghit reached out from the door just in front of Steve and grabbed the berretta. He hit the disassemble lever and took the top of the gun with the barrel off and threw it on the floor.

"You got one of the old berretta's. The new models had that problem fixed."

Steve stood there in stunned amazement at his gun being disassembled in a split second. He looked up at the dark image of Shoeghit standing just feet in front of him.

"You ever been tasered before? It really makes your hair stand up."

Steve tried to lean back fast but Shoeghit was too quick, jabbing the steel prods into his gut and electrifying him. His muscles all flexed at the amperage squeezing his nervous system. He tried to keep his faculties but couldn't, falling to the carpet.

Shoeghit startled him repeatedly jabbing the prods into his back shocking him over and over. Steve cried out in pain, his teeth repeatedly mashing down cutting his tongue. Blood poured from his mouth.

"Yeah, not so much fun being on the receiving end, is it? I bet you thought you were too smart to get caught."

Gasping for breath, Steve with all his strength grabbed Shoeghit's heel and pulled it hard, causing him to fall backward. He crawled out from under him like a rabid animal, diving around the doorway Shoeghit had come out from. The room was completely dark. Steve rolled and rolled to get further into the room.

The haunting figure of Shoeghit stood in the door. "Come back Steve, we're not done yet."

Steve could feel himself bleeding, not only from the mouth but from the hands as well. He had rolled through some of the glass from the broken light bulbs.

"You think you're so smart little man," Shoeghit said into the darkness, "You think you're so smart! Come on, I'm right here. Does the old Jew scare you?" Shoeghit pressed the trigger on the taser and the prods electrified shooting sparks and giving enough illumination to show where Steve was crouched down at the side of the chair. "Now it's my turn, Steve."

With all his might Steve wanted to attack, but his body wasn't responding. That taser really fucked him up. He could barely get to his feet.

In the dim light thrown by the sparking, Steve spotted a set of double doors to the side connecting to another room. He got to his feet, his knees still wobbly and ran for the doors. His faculties still disoriented, he crashed into a porcelain lamp on a table and it smashed on the ground shattering it to pieces.

He could just barely see into the next room. A street light at the end of the block illuminated dim shadows through a shade. He dove to the floor crawling up behind a couch. That was all his legs could take at the moment. Steve cursed angrily at himself. He was usually the pinnacle of fitness even with all his drinking. His body wasn't responding yet.

"Do you know how much pain and suffering you've caused me?" Shoeghit's voice came from behind the wall. He didn't follow Steve into the room.

"Shit," Steve thought to himself. "He's getting a gun." For the first time in years the end looked like it wouldn't be far from now. Thinking back at the struggle and accomplishment, it was a shame he couldn't finish with this being the grand finale, so close to finishing off two of the most powerful people in northern California.

"Your meddling ruined my entire plan. If you hadn't stolen that petty two hundred grand, Frank Ross would be mayor now."

The voice seemed to move in the hall from behind the wall. Steve needed to mark the spot he was at by saying something out loud and then move.

"Well it couldn't of happened to a nicer person. I'm happy to have stuck it to you." He crawled as quietly as he could back to the door he just entered the room from. Instead of putting his back up against the wall, he lay flat to the floor like he was asleep, ear to the ground. Steve figured Shoeghit would be smart enough to shoot through the wall. He listened with all his focus to see if he could hear where his footsteps where coming from. He was sure Shoeghit had a painful death planned for him. He felt almost like crying. Not from feeling sorry for himself, but from losing to someone he detested so very badly. It was similar to the warrior athletes in the super bowl. No one doubted their courage. To get to that level, and then to get to the Super Bowl, but lose. They sometimes angrily cried at being thwarted. The Super Bowl ring within reach then taken back from them.

Hard laughter came from behind the walls. "Ha! Are you there? Listen if you will." Shoeghit was mocking Steve's talents. "Cucktchic," the distinctive sound of the HK5s lever being cocked. "HK5, I prefer the Uzi to this German scrap metal."

The voice sounded closer. Steve was looking at the window wondering if he should chance the two story drop. Not very cool leaving Touw behind to be tortured and killed. Especially after he refused to leave Steve and flee the country. Steve couldn't bring himself to desert his friend, not this time. He would have to live with himself, and the self-imposed disgrace. Steve decided he would rather die this time.

"Ah!" a muffled growl of pain. It was definitely from the other adjacent room. Shoeghit was only feet from him on the other side. "You've made me bleed," Shoeghit exclaimed from behind the wall.

Steve knew he was being bated. He lay completely still flat to the floor looking up at the doorway. He put his hands on the floor in a pushup position so as to be able to pounce upward. He could hear Shoeghit's labored breathing now. The 'plop, plop' sound of liquid hitting the hard wood floor on the other side. He was bleeding bad. Must of really fucked up his hand.

"You're going to die, you're going to die, you're going to die," Shoeghit started softly saying. It was scary and psychotically hypnotic. He was definitely skilled at killing.

Springing to his feet, Steve ran through the room and into the completely dark hall.

"Run! Hahaha! RUN, STEVE!"

In the hall he felt the walls 'til he reached the dead end. There was a door to the left but it was locked.

"Whoooaaa, Stevey. Come back to meeee."

The voice was unnervingly close. Too close. Steve guessed at the door to the hall from the room he just exited. Ten, fifteen feet maybe. One spray from the HK5 in his direction and his life would be over. Forever.

He measured two steps back from the door in the darkness and slammed into it with his shoulder, jarring it hard, but not freeing it.

"That's right, try to stay alive. How are you going to do it? You destroyed me. Now I have nothing to lose." The voice echoed in the hall. "Run Steve." POP! A single shot rang out from the gun lighting the whole hall with the flash, whizzing by Steve's face so close he could feel the vortex of the bullet suck against his skin.

Steve screamed out in a death cry and pummeled himself into the door smashing it open, Crash! It slammed back, wood splinters flying everywhere. His momentum caused him to fall to the floor, but there was no time to be hurt. Springing back up he ran into the completely dark room tipping objects over and falling again.

The huge mansion had a circular design of connecting doors as he could see a tiny bit of light coming from the one connecting back into a room in the main body of the house. He ran straight at it arms crossed over his face bursting through the door with another crash. Light. A lamp was on in the room. A normally dimly-lit room seemed bright compared to the stark darkness Steve had just endured.

Shoeghit's laugh echoed from the room behind him. A stark maddening laugh of a mad killer on the prowl. He was enjoying himself.

No exit from this room Steve realized as his heart stopped. It was like a bad dream where you want to run away but your legs don't move. A decorated slanted forty five degree wood ladder went to a trap door in the roof, but he thought he was on the top floor. Suddenly he remembered the Caufields had a solarium.

Without hesitation Steve rocketed up the steps pushing through the trap door like it wasn't there. The popping noise of the HK5 and whistling bullets ripped chunks out of the heavy ladders rails at his heals.

The cold air of the unheated solarium caught him. Steve grabbed the large telescope and pushed it down the stairs. It crunched and banged all the way to the bottom. The windows didn't open up here and the roof was a sealed bubble.

Shoeghit's voice came from the bottom of the stairs. "You know you can't escape from there. I was going to tell you until you threw the telescope down. You bad boy. Come down now! It's over."

Steve desperately tried to find a way to kick the window out but it was futile. He removed his backpack and threw it to the floor. "OK, Shoeghit, you got me. Why should I come down? Come up here and kill me so the whole neighborhood can see you do it."

A foot stepped onto the bottom of the ladder, it groaned with the weight. "Oh trust me. They can't see you in there."

Steve removed the door shaped charges. They were useless for anything but blowing locks open. He placed one at both sides of the trap door top where the heavy wooden ladder was anchored to it. Frantically Steve connected the wires to the small battery pack.

The noise of Shoeghit's steps grew closer. Steve wrapped the ground around one side of the small battery and then grabbed the hot wire. He crouched as far back as he could, not sure if the charge was set right. If he was off one of the metal sheathes could take his legs off.

Shoeghit grew silent magically again, a real talent of his. Steve couldn't hear anything except a drip of blood falling from his injured hand hitting a step on about four down from the top. Now he coaxed himself before he stuck the gun in and sprayed the place down. Blowing yourself up. Take your enemy with you.

BOOM!

Everything went black for a second as the shaped charge blasted half the floor away. The huge heavy wooden ladder went crashing down to the floor, Shoeghit riding on it. Not sure if he was hurt or not, Steve—in a desperate attempt to save his life—rolled into the smoke letting himself fall through the hole. He fell to the floor below.

Shoeghit was dazed and bloody in the face. He was reaching around for the HK5 which was in front of him a foot from where he had dropped it. Steve leaped up to his feet and stepped up to Shoeghit. He reared back with all his might like a field goal kicker would try an extra point and punted Shoeghit in the head with his boot cold-cocking him. Shoeghit lay out cold on top of the ladder that had fallen to the floor.

Steve stood over Shoeghit staring down at him. Something bumped his shoulder and he turned exhaustedly around, his fist clinched for delivering a blow.

"Easy Boss, just me," Touw said.

"Where in the fuck have you been?"

"I went down to the dock to neutralize the guard."

"Did it occur to you I might need help?" Steve asked whimsically.

"Well, no. You've never been defeated before. Why would it be different today?" Touw smiled.

"Yeah right! Come on, we've got to get out of here."

"Do we have time to make off with a couple million in cash down on the boat?"

Steve looked at him and grew a big grin across his entire face. "Do you know how to sail?"

"Nope, but we're going to learn aren't we?"

"Yep."

10

You needed to have a sense of humor to appreciate two thieves who had never sailed before trying to sail across San Francisco Bay in the darkness. Touw and Steve laughed and giggled as the big sailboat plodded along through the waves. They managed to get one sail up correctly and had enough of a crosswind to keep moving before Steve got the motor started. The stout little chug chug motor had just enough go in it to make its way through the flood tide. Touw wrestled with the sail they had managed to raise and after trying to bring it down twice he just cut it off and let it drop into the ocean.

Steve went around Alcatraz and straight for Pier 45. Everything looked so different from the water. It was hard to tell where you were. Ghiradelli Square stood all lit up behind that particular pier like a beacon. Steve would be sure not to miss it. Twenty minutes went by before they were back in the middle of San Francisco.

Before going into the fish pier, a cell phone call was made to Gena asking her to lock up the RV, making sure to pull all the shades down. Steve told her to calmly walk down the hill and get the war car, then to drive normally over to Pier 45 and meet them.

The forward bedroom of the yacht was where their prize catch was stored along with the bounty. Shoeghit lay on the bed hog-tied. Along with rope, he was also duct-taped across the mouth, over the eyes, and around the knees. Houdini couldn't have gotten out of the restraints.

They moored the boat as best they could without waking the sleeping fishermen. A solid crunch on one of the pilings cracked something up front but Steve didn't bother to look. Touw jumped up to the dock and tied the lines off. No one seemed to notice among the boats at mooring except a crusty old Vietnamese fisherman who asked Touw how long they would be moored there. The fisherman needed to off-load his catch within an hour or so. Touw assured him they would be long gone in the morning. The fisherman assumed he meant with the boat and went back below on his vessel.

Shortly Gena showed up with the war car sporting a broken back window and some blood on the door they had failed to notice earlier. Touw pointed it out to Steve silently before wiping it off.

With precision, the motivated thieves off-loaded the boat in less than three minutes and were on their way back to the RV. Not one word was said in the drive back over crossing the

Golden Gate Bridge again. Upon returning, the entire crew loaded back into the RV, keeping the shades down.

"We're filthy rich!" Touw finally broke the silence. He just plopped Shoeghit in the middle of the floor and stepped over him.

"We did it, Babe," Steve said giving Touw a big hug.

"I want to see what's happening at the mansion," Touw said, walking to the back room of the Winnebago and peering out the large binoculars on the tripod.

"Well, what's the story?" Steve asked while giving Gena a big aggressive embrace.

"The story is five cop cars. A coroner's van and a couple of news trucks."

"I'm not picking up anything on the scanners."

"No, not at the house," Touw's voice billowed out excitedly from the back room. "They found the private patrol."

"Oh, him. He deserved what he got."

"Yeah, by the way, great idea about bugging the crime scene before we left."

Gena said curiously, "Why did you bug the house afterwards?"

"So we could monitor the investigation, know how much they know. We'll be able to stay one step ahead of them, and they won't have a clue how. We'll know if they think it's us, as well."

"Well, they haven't discovered the house yet. I'm sure of it. The officers are totally engrossed in the outside incident."

"Good," Steve responded, "People hated the Caulfields. Nobody's going to be in any hurry to check on them. Just look at the walls surrounding the house. You call that being a friendly neighbor? Not hardly. What comes around goes around, and they got theirs."

Steve paused for a second thinking, stroking his beard with his hand. "Why don't we move the RV out of the area and get some breakfast. I'm famished. Anybody for some steak and eggs?"

"That's a big ten four," Touw exclaimed coming out of the back room.

Gena didn't look as happy as Steve and Touw. She asked, "What do we do now? Do we have to flee the country? They still want to arrest us you know."

"No. I told you sweetie, this time you're with the right man." Steve smiled with a big trusting grin. "I will take care of everything."

Touw listened in along with Gena.

"The plan is this..."

******

Touw and Steve proceeded to store all the equipment, stashing things in new places in case they were compromised. They cut Gena loose to track down Ivan. She could move around a lot more easily without them. The young crowd wouldn't think anything of her asking where her ex was. But if they picked up on a couple of older gentleman tagging along they might not help her out.

It was four in the afternoon on Wednesday when Gena finally checked in. Sure enough she had found them down at the Eden Hotel. They checked in late last night and hadn't been seen since going into their room. Their rent was up this morning and the manager was going to roust them out. Steve insisted that Gena persuade the manager to let them stay longer. He told her to pay them up for two more days and make sure she got a key. Touw and Steve were on their way.

Mission Street in San Francisco was accustomed to seeing anything from people laying in the gutter, to fist fights breaking out in the middle of the street. So it wasn't that much of a big deal to see someone carrying another person over their shoulder which is how Steve towed Shoeghit into the hotel. They had unbound him after heavily drugging him with Touw's sister's sleeping pill prescription.

Behind the cage this time was the hag from hell, a cigarette hanging from her lips, low cut five-and-dime blouse unbuttoned to reveal her bony protruding collar bone going to where her breasts would have been hanging ten years ago.

The sun was burning brightly through the dirty Plexiglas windows in the front of the hotel. The un-air-conditioned front lobby was sweltering.

Steve approached the window with the little silver ashtray-sized hole in it with Shoeghit slung over his shoulder. The gruff old lady spoke before he could say anything.

"You're not bringing him in here! We have enough trouble."

"Oh, no, ma'am. We're no trouble. We're friends of Gena."

"Gena, my sweetheart! What did she get into this time."

Steve pointed with his thumb of his free hand, "This is her uncle."

The old hag broke out laughing in a raspy cigarette coughing laugh. They were speaking her language now.

"We just want to stay for an hour. We can't leave her uncle in the car with all this heat. We would have to leave the windows down, and you know this neighborhood." Steve nodded, smiling and stroking his beard slightly.

The hag was noticeably turned on by Steve's burly mountain-man appearance. He was a little more unkept than normal from all the running around.

"Come on in honey," she declared, buzzing the doors. They opened to the small hallway past the office. At the end of the narrow hall, the stairs disappeared up into the labyrinth of the old hotel.

The stench created by the heat was even worse than usual. The stagnant air surrounded them. The old gal at the window opened the half-door on the side of the office connecting to the hall. She reached out and grabbed Steve by the shoulder sleeve causing him to jump, startled slightly.

She talked in a rattling-on style, "They're not in the third floor suite this time. He just had a little money and I'm tired of covering him so I put him in the first floor single room."

She kept babbling so Steve turned to face her out of courtesy, bumping Shoeghit's head on the wall in the process. Touw snickered at Steve's carelessness.

"Yeah," the old hag kept going, "If he has to puke, put him in the community bathroom in the middle hall. Stick his head in the toilet. They're clean, he won't get cooties. I don't want to have to come up there to clean up any barf, you hear. Room 104. If I have to clean a mess, Gena will be forced to pay an extra deposit next time."

"No problem," Steve assured the old lady. "We'll take care of everything," he said, winking his crystal blue eyes at her and smiling. He manhandled Shoeghit up the stairs to the second floor.

Touw plugged his nose while following, "God, this place reeks. "

At the door Steve knocked twice, stepping off to the side. Touw put his hand on the butt of the pistol tucked into his pants under his shirt. Gradually the latch unhitched and the door cracked open. Gena peeked out first and then opened it wider so they could come in.

"I brought a present," Steve said.

"I see that. Enter please."

As he squeezed through the door into the room he sized up the space. "Good grief, what a mess."

Touw entered the room shutting the door behind him. He placed his finger on his nose to hold his nostrils shut.

Steve smiled and laughed, "What's the matter, Touw? Don't you like these cheap hotels?"

"Not for me," Touw replied.

This small room had an old bed with a cheap bedspread on it. An old dresser drawer under two windows looked out onto Mission Street.

"Gena, pull those shades," Steve said.

The old shades barely came down far enough to cover all the light coming in the windows. They were all bent and mangled. Gena adjusted them as best she could. The bed had been broken into two different pieces. The box spring and the mattress spread out onto the floor. Ivan was sound asleep oblivious to anyone, and Dilan was face down on the mattress sleeping in his puke that he had regurgitated.

"They don't even know we're here," Steve expounded.

"No they don't," Gena answered. "They go on these two and three day speed trips and then sleep for an entire day. But it looks like with all the excitement, they went on a four day binge. I found ATM receipts from four days ago.

Steve looked the place over and smiled an evil grin. "Well let's see... Where do we want to put Shoeghit?"

The old gangster hung limp over Steve's shoulder, still out cold from a double dose of sleeping pills. They had borrowed the pills from Touw's sister who was an insomniac. Steve hoisted Shoeghit down from his shoulder holding him in front of his chest. He then set Shoeghit down in the pool of vomit that Dilan had regurgitated out onto the mattress.

"Ah, a fitting end to my mortal enemy." Steve pushed him down into the puke a little harder, rubbing his face back and forth. He removed the duct-tape from his pocket and retaped his mouth, hands, and legs thoroughly.

"OK, a note. Ahh...note." Steve mumbled to himself looking around the room. He ripped a piece of the phonebook cover off and took out a felt pen.

"Dear Ivan, my friend that has caused me so much grief. Please accept my gift of Bill Shoeghit, a millionaire capitalist pig as your prisoner. This should absolve me for all my capitalist crimes. And in your pursuit of anarchism please don't hold any grudges with your fellow comrades in crime, The Listener Thieves. For I am the Thieves' Guild Master who presents you this gift. I'm sure our paths will cross again in the future.

PS. In case you missed the news in your drugged-out blur, there is a hundred thousand dollar reward for the capture of this gentleman who lays in your vomit. If you take it upon yourself to turn him in for this reward, you will not be looked down upon in any way. Although it would contradict your anarchist pipe dream, I'm sure you would find some use for the money. Yours truly, The Listener Thieves."

Steve took the back cover of the phone book and tucked it into the front of Ivan's shirt. Ivan the Terrible, I see. More like Ivan the terribly fucked-up. This way when he woke up he couldn't help but have to pull it out. It was screw-up proof. Steve just hoped he would notice to read it.

Then he gave Shoeghit one more symbolic

kick in the ribs to ensure he was out cold. Shoeghit didn't respond.

"Gena, how long do you think these two will sleep like this?"

"Mmm, let's see," she calculated it like a math equation. "Up for four days. Sleep for a day and a half. Wake up totally dehydrated and starved to death. Once they get water and food they'll be OK."

"Do they have any money?"

"Nope wallets are empty, just ATM receipts from their four-day binge."

"OK, better give them some money. Don't want them to panhandle before turning Shoeghit in." Steve grabbed his money clip and peeled off two hundred dollars and stuck it into Ivan's pants.

"Do you think they'll turn in Shoeghit, or do you think they will just kill him?"

"Or do you think they'll let him go," Touw interjected, breaking his silence.

"Oh, I have a sneaky suspicion they will turn him in. I have faith in the power of capitalism. I never believed a true anarchist exists. It's just a cheap crutch for poor to give a well deserved shot in the ribs to the rich. If I was a betting man, and I am, that reward will be claimed by tomorrow afternoon. Is there a back way out of this hotel? I don't want to go by the hag again. I think she likes me.

"Yes," Gena said, "There's a side fire exit to the alley. But there's a switch that sets off the fire alarm when you open it."

Smiling a sinister grin Steve said, "Show me the exit. I think we can handle it."

******

Sitting on the tarmac at San Francisco International Airport in his helicopter, Steve thumbed the switches energizing the power systems. The 'copter began charging up, ready for the turbines to start. He smiled at Gena buckling into the passenger side seat and picked up his phone. Reading the number to the police chief's private phone off the clip board in his lap he waited for an answer.

"Hello, Officer Romy."

"Yes, Officer Romy, I would like to talk to the police chief. I was informed that this was the phone number to his cellular phone."

"I'm sorry Chief McHale's not available. May I take a message?"

"Yes, it's imperative that I talk to him, and I won't be leaving a number to return the call. I'm a news reporter, and I'm running a story on a secretary that died under mysterious circumstances. We're printing in one hour, and we want to know if the chief wishes to defend himself against the accusation. The accusation is murder."

Silence on the line for a minute, followed by some whispers.

"Yes, this is Chief Ken McHale."

"Ah yes Chief. We're an interested party in the events of the past days. So let's cut straight to the point, Chief. You serve at the pleasure of the mayor. Am I correct on that?"

"Who is this? What's this about?"

"I'm an interested party in your political future. Did you or did you not have a secretary go missing in the past?"

"Yes, but it was an accidental death."

"Yes of course, investigated by you...right?"

The chief stumbled over his words not knowing how to respond.

Steve spoke confidently into the phone, "OK. One. You serve at the pleasure of the mayor. Mayor's dead. Looks good that the chief of staff's going to be the next mayor. Who am I? I'm the person that broke into Frank Ross's safe. I bet you don't know about that. It went unreported for obvious reasons. This is basically how the whole show got started."

The chief silently listened like any good cop would at someone incriminating himself.

"A bit of interesting information was acquired pertaining to you, from Frank Ross's personal safe. The information was provided to Frank

Ross by the chief of staff, now mayor, Richard Morris. There are extensive notes made pertaining to your secretary threatening you with sexual harassment. I'm reading them as we speak. Would you care for me to recite them over the open air waves or do you feel confident that I know what I'm talking about."

"No, that's fine. Go on with what you have to say," the chief responded, sounding disheartened.

"OK, this is what we're going to do for you, Chief. One, Shoeghit. The entire city is looking for him."

Steve decided he wasn't going to take a chance on a bunch of tweaker junkies screwing things up.

Shoeghit's in the Eden Hotel, room 104 right now. He's tied up, so you won't need the SWAT team. Make the collar yourself. You'll look good.

Two. See that the two crackhead idiots in there with him, passed out, get the reward. Pump them up, get them a press agent. Whatever you got to do. Hero them. The press does it all the time.

Three. You serve at the pleasure of the mayor. The mayor has the option to appoint a new police chief upon victory. Am I correct on that?"

"Yes that's correct," the chief said.

"Well, Richard Morris is a shoe-in to win this election on Friday. He will want to remove you as chief, which we don't want to happen at this time. We want you as a counter balance to his power. So following this conversation I will make a phone call to the new mayor and dictate our concern that you remain as chief. You are to keep your job in a prestigious manner, and he is to give his full enthusiasm to your next four years as chief. We will make this so. Do you have confidence in our abilities?"

"Yes, I do," the chief said softly into the phone.

"Fine," Steve said. "Follow through on picking up Shoeghit. You may never hear from us again, but if you ever receive a call as chief from a party with the initials LT, you will be expected to take it immediately."

The chief responded in a relatively upbeat mood. "That will not be a problem."

"Enjoy your next four years, Chief. Goodbye," Steve said confidently into the phone. He then disconnected.

Immediately upon hanging up, Steve engaged the turbines starter, and the whine of the powerful gas turbines took over. The rotor started spinning faster and faster 'til it reached its supersonic speed. He lifted off, tilting the nose down and headed for the sea.

At the coast Steve turned north and set his auto pilot at five hundred feet. He dialed in a radio frequency to the overhead radio and removed the mike from the console. "Touw, are you ready?"

"Yes, let's do this and get out of here. I'm tired of this crap. I want to get started on my vacation."

"Sounds good to me. Stand by."

Steve let the mike hang down so he didn't have to reach up again. He then picked up the cellular phone, dialing the mayor's office direct line to his personal security.

After ringing once it was picked up and answered by a lady's voice. "Mayor's office."

"Give me the mayor, please."

"May I ask who's calling?"

"Give him this message directly please. It's the concerned party that has direct knowledge of the contents of Frank Ross's safe. Including information provided by him to the opposition on the chief of police."

"Yes, sir. Please hold," she said, almost matter of fact.

Steve looked out the window of the cockpit at the beautiful California coast line. Hundreds of people out enjoying the beach, waves crashing down on the white sparkly sand. He cranked up some rock and roll on the stereo to drown out the rotor noise.

"Yes. Mayor Richard Morris. How may I help you?" The mayor was sitting in his office surrounded by a plethora of private security listening in on the speaker phone. One had a radio to a van parked in front of City Hall with a number of antennas on the roof. One member of the security team motioned with his hands to spread the conversation out as long as possible.

"We're concerned with your bid to be mayor. We want to get a few things straight before you take office."

"And why should I listen to you?" the mayor said back sarcastically.

"How about the fact that you gave information about the police chief to the opposition to ensure your job security?"

"Why should that concern me? I was not the conspirator of that crime. I merely recorded the facts. It's his problem. He should stand up for what he's done."

Steve face turned angry. "Listen you son of a bitch," he yelled into the phone loudly. "The only reason you're mayor is because we say you are. I just got rid of your boss and the people that ran against him. You want to piss me off? You think you're bad now? The chief of police, whom you were going to sell out in case your boy lost, is running an investigation on you. Would you care for him to find out that the woman murdered in the Japantown garage was at your house the night before? Should we check for DNA? Also, she was at City Hall during the shooting. Should we open this wound up? How about we start tomorrow, Thursday, the day before the election."

"No, no don't do that," Richard Morris said into the phone passively. He looked up at his security team. One whispered into the walky-talky to find if the call has been traced yet.

"Oh, by the way. Are you trying to trace this call?" Steve grabbed the mike. "Now!" he said into his radio.

Boom, boom, boom, boom, four shots rang out from a long distance away. The window in front of the van shattered and the radiator sprayed out water from the Russian sniper rifle's bullets. Two men threw open the sliding door and scrambled to the ground, narrowly escaping the bullets slamming through the vehicle.

Touw keyed his mike "done," as he already had his rifle disassembled and stuffed into a back pack.

"Oh, what happened smart guy? That kind've spoiled your plans I guess."

"All right. No more killing please. I beg you."

"You know who's boss now, right?"

"Yes."

"My initials are LT. You take orders from me if you want to be mayor."

"OK."

"Enjoy your term in office. I won't be coming

to your inauguration."

Richard wiped the sweat off his forehead. "Sure whatever you say."

Click Steve hung up the phone. He looked out his window to be sure his skis were securely fastened to the helicopters skids.

"Is that it? Are we done?" Gena asked.

"Yes, we're all done. Let's go to Tahoe."

"Yeah!" Gena yelled out joyously. She popped the cork on a bottle of champagne then leaned across and gave Steve a tremendous kiss. "I love you, Listener Thief."